THE KRINAR'S
INFORMANT

A Krinar World Novel

CHARMAINE PAULS

Published by Charmaine Pauls

Montpellier, 34090, France

www.charmainepauls.com

Published in France

Cover design by Najla Qamber Designs

(www.najlaqamberdesigns.com)

ISBN: 978-2956103172 (eBook)

ISBN-13: 978-1727761429 (Print)

ISBN-10: 1727761421 (Print)

❀ Created with Vellum

Chapter One

The jungle resonated with sounds of night creatures, sounds Liv never heard on the footpath in the shady light of day. She ducked as a giant ghost bat swooped low, the large span of its wing brushing her hair. Shivering, she hugged herself and trudged forward, keeping her gaze on the path for snakes. A moving shadow on a tree trunk caught her eye. A tarantula scurried over the bark. She barely missed head butting the cocoon suspended on silky strings that stretched between two branches. Glowing silver in the moonlight, the semi-transparent cocoon vibrated, sending a ripple through the web. Something struggled inside, something bulky and black. She refused to think of its content.

This was for Erik and Karl.

If her brothers discovered her gone, they'd be furious. She didn't even want to think what Hans would do to her, but there was no other way. She had to meet the Krinar, and the village on the outskirts of the jungle was the only public place within walking distance. Even if Anita said she could trust him, she wasn't going to risk being alone with an alien who'd single-handedly wiped out armies of Resistance fighters.

Steeling herself, she continued on her journey, the hair on her arms rising with every crack of a branch and hoot of an owl. She was used to the flat, open expanses of the Kalahari Desert. Sand she could handle. Reptiles and hairy jungle insects not so much. Soon, the soles of her hiking boots were caked with mud, losing traction and making her slip on the moss-covered rocks. Humidity dampened her clothes. The long-sleeved shirt didn't do much to protect her against the mosquitos, either. They were nothing short of vampires, stinging through the lightweight fabric.

When distant lights became visible through the dense vegetation, she exhaled in relief and picked up her pace. She'd chosen the bar. Except for a few houses and a grocery store, there was no place else. Standing on the step of the open door, she surveyed the space. Men in dirty vests threw daggers at a target drawn on the wooden wall. A rowdy group downed shooters at the counter. A man with oily hair and a shiny face looked up. Maybe the bar wasn't such a good idea. How could she have known? She'd never been on this side of the jungle. It was too late. They'd already spotted her. If she fled, it would be like turning one's back on a lion—an open invitation to attack. False bravery was her best defense.

Lifting her chin, she walked inside and took her time to decide on the best spot. Two chairs in a corner were vacant. She was about to take one when the man with the oily hair sauntered over.

"Hello, sweetness," he said with a Spanish accent.

"I'm not your sweetness."

He grinned. "You will be."

Without warning, his hand shot out, gripping her braid. He gave a pluck, jerking her closer.

She winced at the sting on her scalp. "Let go."

He chuckled. "Or?"

"Or you become a eunuch," a deep voice said from the door.

The whole bar's attention turned toward the sound.

A giant, as muscled as he was tall, stood in the doorway. His face was sculptured in angular lines, his jaw square, and his nose straight. A neatly trimmed beard drew attention to those lines, making his face seem harder. His dark hair was cropped close to his skull in the military style her brothers favored. Red welts on his upper arms marred the even tone of his bronze skin. The wounds looked fresh. As his slate-gray eyes landed on the foul-smelling man's hand where it was fisted in her hair, they flashed with a spark too otherworldly to be human. There was no mistaking the physical perfection and unusual size. He was a Krinar. The bar had gone silent. The man next to her was frozen to the spot.

The K stepped over the threshold. With a wide stance, he took in the room much as she'd done upon her arrival. He appeared docile, but experience had taught her that men with a calm demeanor were often the most dangerous. His attire was in the lighter colors the Ks in Lenkarda favored. Khaki pants molded over powerful thighs, and a beige, sleeveless T-shirt stretched over his broad chest. Every hard contour of his muscles was visible under the fabric.

Her mouth went dry. Did she do the right thing? The K was a killing machine, a Resistance hunter, and she was with the Resistance. He was lion. She was prey. The only thing that guaranteed her safety was the information she could provide. He wasn't going to rip her limbs off before he'd gotten intel. Was he?

The man who held her uttered a surprised curse and looked at his crotch. She followed his gaze. The flip knife in her hand indented his jean-covered testicles. With the K throwing her off-balance, she hadn't realized how much pressure she was applying.

The K chuckled. "As I said, you're about to lose your balls." He tilted his head. "Or maybe your dick. Women can be unpredictable."

The man released her and took a step back. She resisted the urge to massage the sore spot on her skull, instead focusing all her attention on the K who moved deeper into the bar with lithe strides. Too fast and agile, neither she nor the man could predict his path until he was in the face of her molester.

"You touched my *date*."

The man threw his hands up. "Hey, man, I didn't know. No hard feelings."

The K looked down at the man as if he was examining a bug. "Oh, but you're wrong. There are hard feelings. Plenty."

The man didn't wait. He stumbled two steps back, knocked over a chair, and ran for the door.

The K gave her a once-over. "Do you want me to go after him?"

She swallowed. "I had it under control."

He smirked. "I noticed." Picking up the chair, he placed it in front of her. "Sit." His grin stretched wider. "Put the knife away first."

Only when she'd pocketed the knife and flopped down on the seat did he take the chair on the opposite side of the table. Grateful for the distance, however small, she exhaled the breath she was holding, trying to calm her erratic breathing.

The K leaned back, scrutinizing her. "You must be Liv." He said the name slowly, as if he was testing the sound on his tongue.

A waitress slid up to them, her eyes darting toward the bar where the bartender was shooing her on with his hands. She pulled down the hem of her tank top, trying to cover her stomach.

"What can I get you?" she asked in a high-pitched voice.

Poor girl. Liv knew how she felt. Under the table, her knees were shaking. "Nothing for me, thank you."

"You're in a bar," the K said. "You're occupying one of their chairs. You have to order something. Isn't that the rule?"

She was too nervous to drink. "I'm fine, really."

"Mineral water with a slice of lemon for my *date*," he said, "and a fruit juice for me. Anything in season. Freshly squeezed. No ice."

Wait a minute. How did he know what she drank? An uneasy shudder ran down her spine.

"Sure," the waitress squeaked. She scurried away as fast as she could without making it obvious that she was running.

Liv didn't blame her. The alien's voice was commanding. He made it sound as if failure came with a death warrant, even for something as trivial as accidently putting ice cubes in his juice. If the way he ordered drinks was so assertive, what was he like in combat? She pushed the disturbing thought aside.

"Would you like something to eat, *date*?"

Despite the air of danger surrounding him, the K's choice of words was starting to grind on her.

"Just so we're clear," she said, "I'm not your date. I know there's a language barrier, so I'll excuse you for the innocent mistake. Maybe your translator chip is malfunctioning."

A wicked glint played in his eyes. "My *chip* works fine. There's no mistake or innocence on my part." He arched a perfect brow. "We're ordering drinks in a bar. Isn't that the definition of a date?"

Was he making fun of her? "I'm not here to play games."

He leaned closer, his gaze penetrating. "You think I am?" A slow smile curved his lips. "I do play, Miss Madsen, but not games."

She reeled at the intensity in his strange eyes, her breath catching on a silent gasp. The waitress appeared with their drinks, not giving her time to analyze the statement.

Stay on track. Follow the plan. Breathe.

Anita had said the K who'd help her was a good, solid soldier, a guardian both Korum and Mia respected. Anita liked him. She'd gone as far as to say he was like the brother she never had. It couldn't be the arrogant alien facing her. Anita would never approve of such an attitude.

She waited until the waitress was gone before she asked, "You are Zavir, right?"

"Would I be here if I wasn't?"

It could be a set-up. He could be a Keith, a K working with the Resistance. With Resistance movements popping up faster than mushrooms around the globe, there was so much backstabbing going on one could never be sure.

He pushed the water toward her and picked up his own glass. No ice. *Thank God.*

"Drink," he said. "You appear dehydrated."

She chose to ignore the diagnosis, even if her lips were parched. "I'll need to see some ID."

His disturbing eyes widened a fraction, and then his smile turned mocking. "Of course, you do."

Taking his time, he pulled up a hologram from a wristwatch device. His credentials hovered in the space between them.

"Any Krinar can fake an ID. I want proof."

He crossed his arms and leaned back, looking like he was getting comfortable to watch a sitcom. Do Ks even watch comedies? Do they share the same sense of humor?

"What proof do you have in mind?" he asked with a lazy drawl.

"Anita said you have a birthmark."

All pretense of friendliness vanished from his tone. "A defect, you mean."

"Show it to me."

His eyes tightened. "Anita, as in Wian's charl?"

"Yes."

"How are you acquainted?"

"We're friends. We met in South Africa while we were both on holiday in Cape Town. It was Anita who suggested I get in touch with Korum. Korum told me he'd set up a meeting with you. When I asked how I could be sure it was you, he told me about your mark."

"You trust Korum."

"Of course. I know Mia. If she trusts him enough to live with him, so do I."

He gave her a calculated look. "Did he tell you where this mark is?"

She swallowed but squared her shoulders. "Yes."

Amusement returned. "I guess we should step outside, then."

"I'm not going anywhere with you until I know you're Zavir for sure."

"All right, little human. Suit yourself."

Holding her eyes, his mocking smile turned wider as his hands went to the waistband of his pants. She swallowed a couple of times more while he unbuttoned, but she didn't blink an eye, not even when he lifted his hips to work the fabric an inch down his ass. She leaned over the table to examine the red mark that started at the top of his pelvic bone and disappeared along the line of his groin. Upon her insistence, Korum had sent her a simulation of the mark. There should be small half-moon a fraction lower to the right.

"More," she said.

For a second, he seemed surprised, but then his look turned into something she couldn't place, something challenging.

"Who am I to deny a pretty lady?"

The pants slipped farther down his thighs, revealing the hard V that cut from his hips, but also the top of his male parts, his very large, hardening male parts.

"Stop," she said in a jerky voice, but not before his cock had thickened more.

"Are you sure about that, little human? I can give you all the proof you want."

What a jerk. He *was* messing with her, and it wasn't the kind of messing designed to put her at ease.

Deciding no reaction was the best reaction, she said, "We can't talk in here."

"Then why did you want to meet here?"

"You didn't think I was going to meet you alone without first establishing you're the real Zavir?"

"Do you think the men in this bar would stop me if I wanted to kill you?"

"Probably not but ripping my throat out in public will be all over the news. Interspecies relations are fragile as it is. You don't want to risk a scandal that could compromise your Council's mission."

"What do you know of our Council's mission?"

"What Mia told me."

"That is?"

"That they prefer a peaceful transition."

"What prevents me from *ripping out your throat* once I've got you alone?"

Her back turned stiff. "Are you threatening me?" Her words were full of bravado, but her hands shook in her lap.

His deep voice adopted a seductive tone. "It depends on what you perceive as a threat."

Enough. He was a first-class ass. She didn't care how good Korum said he was, she wasn't dealing with him.

"This was a mistake." She stood. "I want someone else."

About to turn, a big hand clamped around her wrist. Her heart slammed in her chest. The chair scraped over the floor as he pushed to his feet. Craning her neck to meet his eyes across the table, it took every ounce of willpower she had not to cower under his dominating height and angry scowl.

"You're stuck with me," he said. "There will be no one else."

"I don't appreciate being threatened," her gaze dropped to where his fingers gripped her, "or harassed."

His hold increased marginally. "That wasn't a threat, and if I was harassing you, my hand wouldn't be on your wrist. It would be somewhere way more tantalizing."

She yanked to free herself, but to no avail. "If this isn't a threat, what do you call it?"

"Education. Teaching you how lame your plan is so you won't make the same stupid mistakes in the future."

"Stupid?" Indignation mixed with her fear. She jerked her arm again, harder this time. "Let go."

Instead of obliging, he picked up the water and held the glass to her lips. "Drink."

She had no choice but to part her lips when he tipped the glass or risk looking like Miss Wet T-shirt in Scumbag Bar. The cool liquid slipped down her throat. Fine, it tasted like heaven, even if she had to admit it rather grudgingly. It was a welcome relief from the dryness in her mouth and the humid heat.

"That's better," he said when she'd downed everything, catching a drop on her bottom lip with his thumb.

Not expecting it, she jumped at his touch.

Coming around the table, he dragged her closer. With their faces inches apart, she could make out the strange slate color of his eyes. What looked like a flat, dark hue from far was a striking mixture of fine-grained gray, deep green, and bluish-purple. Those eyes, so intently fixed on her, were alert and observant. Light shimmered at their depths, making it seem as if they were being illuminated from within. Beautifully frightening.

"What are you doing?" she exclaimed.

"Making this look like a date."

Before she could digest his meaning, he lowered his head and brushed his lips over her ear. She pushed on his shoulders, trying to put distance between them, but his free hand pressed her back to his chest, keeping her in a steel grip.

"Don't fight me," he whispered. "It turns me on."

That made her freeze.

"Look around," he said soft enough for only her to hear. "Every dick in this place will assume you're a tattletale, unless we make it look like a…" his teeth grazed her earlobe, "…date."

The shiver that ran over her was uncontainable. Zavir had felt it, because he chuckled from deep in his chest. Glancing over his broad shoulder, she hated to admit he was right. Every man was staring.

"Put your arms around my neck," he instructed.

She hesitated.

His fingers splayed over her back, taking up an alarmingly big portion of skin. "You do know how to make it look real?"

She shot him an irritated look. "Of course, I do."

He laughed softly. "So brave." His voice dropped an octave, sounding darker and more dangerous. "Now kiss me like you mean it."

"What?" she cried out in shock.

"Kiss me, little human," his wicked voice teased, "so that we have an excuse to take our discussion outside."

She was about to retort with a clever remark, but he didn't give her an opportunity. The moment her lips parted, his mouth slanted over hers. There was nothing tentative about the kiss. His tongue speared past her lips as she gasped. He sucked and molded, not giving her the choice to return or resist the kiss.

His mouth was cool, but his touch seared. Heat built in her chest and spread to her belly. His fingers tightened on her skin while his free hand found purchase in her hair. Her knees turned weak when the heat transformed into something deeper, something that made her breasts tighten and her sex swell. Blood gushed in her ears. Somewhere in the back of her mind, warning bells competed with the deafening thump of her pulse and heart.

What the heck was she doing? This wasn't part of the plan. When she finally came to her senses and tried to push away again, his hand smoothed down her back to cup her ass. She barely bit back a whimper. Her response to his uninvited touch was pathetic. How embarrassing. If he didn't stop, she'd have no pride left. Her only salvation was that he brought the kiss to a slow halt.

His lips brushed her jaw, his breath scorching the shell of her ear. "*Now* we can take it outside."

If he hadn't held onto her when he pulled away, she would've stumbled. In an effort to maintain some resemblance of dignity, or at least the pretense that she was still in charge of her body and sanity, she straightened her clothes. When she fished a bill from her pocket, his large hand closed around hers.

"Drinks are on me," he said. "Isn't that how the *game* works?"

Pulling free, she muttered under her breath, "Instead of mentioning your birthmark, Korum could've simply told me you're obnoxious."

"Careful." He pointed at his ear. "Enhanced hearing, darling."

Perplexed, she allowed him to pull her outside with his vice-like fingers locked around her wrist after he'd taken care of the bill.

The minute they hit the darkness of night, however, she pushed away from him. "How dare you?"

The infuriating bastard didn't bother to answer. He only turned his back on her and disappeared around the building.

"Hey!" She had a childish urge to stamp her foot. "Where are you going?"

With no choice but to follow, she went in the same direction to find him leaning against a tree, his boot propped up against the trunk.

"Let's hear it," he said in an almost bored tone when she stopped in front of him.

Obnoxious, scary, damn alien. How she wished she could kick his ass. "I want my family's safety guaranteed."

He clicked his tongue. "So demanding."

His gaze roamed over her chest and hips.

"If this is a trade-off, aren't you going to tell me first what you have to offer?"

Suggestive bastard. Swallowing an insult, she said, "Information on the biggest Resistance cell the world is yet to see."

He cocked a brow. "The biggest, eh?"

"That's what I said." She couldn't resist a jibe. "You really should have that chip checked out."

He only grinned. "How big?"

"Thousands."

"Here, in Costa Rica?" He sounded doubtful.

"They're spread around the world, but their leader is here. The local group is only a few hundred strong. I'm not only talking numbers, but also power. Think senators, religious opinion leaders." She dropped her voice to a whisper. "Presidents."

His arm muscles flexed as they tightened across his chest. "You have the names?"

"I have better. I have proof."

Gray eyes narrowed. "Weapons?"

"They have scientists on their side. I don't know what they're working on, but I know it will be big. It's supposed to catch you unaware, when you least expect it."

"Can you get this information?"

"Yes. I can also tell you all the cities they plan to attack."

"Why work from here and not one of your big cities, like New York or London?"

"Because they plan to bring down Lenkarda first."

The K stilled. "Impossible. Our defense system is too advanced."

"You're mistaken. Your protective shield can be destroyed."

He moved so quickly she jumped. The one minute he was slumped against the tree, and the next he was in her face. "What's your role in this movement?"

"My brothers are second-in-command to the leader."

He towered over her, his gaze boring into hers. "You'd betray them?"

"Not betray them. Save them. My brothers," she licked her dry lips, "are on a suicide mission."

Chapter Two

"They all are," said the fragile human with the enticing smell of flowers in her hair.

Zavir watched her closely, but her beautiful blue eyes gave away no signs of lies. She held his gaze steadily and kept her back straight.

"This is a war they can't win," she continued. "Besides, the information they're being fed is nothing but propaganda. I don't believe you're here to wipe us out." Her musical voice turned soft. "Are you?"

"If we wanted to wipe you out, we'd have already done so. Where is this information coming from?"

"I'm not saying more until we strike a deal."

He had to smile at her braveness. So much attitude for such a small creature. "Fine, little human. State your conditions."

"I'll give you names, cities, plans, and proof. Everything. All I ask in return is that you guarantee my family's safety and freedom. If you take us down, it must be without bloodshed. I don't want *any* lives lost."

"That's a tall order."

She stood straighter. "Take it or leave it."

Wiping a hand over his chin, he battled not to smile. This tiny creature amused him, and he was *never* amused.

"Fine," he said after stretching the moment out with another few seconds. He was reluctant to end their meeting. It was too much fun. "I'll meet your conditions if you keep your end of the bargain. If not, all bets are off."

She stuck out a dainty hand. "Deal."

His fingers closed around hers. Her skin was soft and warm, her bones fragile. He liked the silky feel. He wanted to trace his palm up her arm and down her side to cup one of those curves that had been teasing him since he'd set foot in the bar. He wanted to ask her to kiss him again.

"Deal," he echoed instead. "How will you get the information?"

"Let me worry about that," she said with a smile way too sweet for where his thoughts were going. "When shall our next meeting be?"

"How soon can you get the information?"

"Tomorrow."

"We need a medium of communication."

She shook her dark hair. "Too dangerous. If they find anything on me, I'm finished. Let's meet back here, same time tomorrow night."

"I should be able to fit it into my schedule," he said with a wink.

Her gaze went to the welts on his shoulder. When her eyes widened, he looked at what she was staring. The wounds had fully healed. He was about to tell her the nanocytes in his body were responsible for the miracle, when his advanced hearing picked up approaching footsteps. Before the shadow had fallen from around the corner of the bar, he'd reversed positions with Liv, pushing her up against the tree while placing his body like a shield in front of her. With his enhanced olfactory ability warning him of the sulphuric smell of gunpowder, his only intention was protecting his newly appointed informant from potential danger, but her proximity seduced every one of his advanced senses at the same time the nearing steps confirmed the owner was a man of short height and meager weight, and the swagger in his step that he was most definitely drunk. Keeping one eye on the danger, he couldn't help but lean closer to his target, caging her between his arms.

"What are you doing?" she asked in alarm.

He dragged his nose along the column of her neck. "Shh. Someone's coming."

A hiccup sounded, and a second later a man stumbled from the side of the building toward the border of the jungle. The buckle of his belt was undone. He was probably just going for a piss, but Zavir couldn't pull himself away from the smell or softness of the skin in front of him. The memory of how her lips had molded under his made him hard all over again, and for a split-second he imagined he could hear the blood coursing through the delicate vein that pulsed in her neck. She lured him, the little siren, seducing him with her vixen attitude and womanly smell. *Just one little taste.* He flicked his tongue along the curve of her neck, down to her shoulder. The shiver rippling through her didn't escape him. Neither did the moan she bit back too late, and then everything went haywire.

His hips rocked forward, drawn to the soft spot between her thighs like a pod to a magnetic landing patch. His fingers clutched at her breasts, grabbing two hands full. His tongue traced her skin, tasting the sweetness of it. It was like a drug. He couldn't get enough. The pissing man was all but forgotten as Zavir rubbed up against Liv like a lovesick dog.

"What are you doing?" she cried out again.

"Giving you an authentic-looking reason for being out here with me," he lied.

"Zavir, we must stop."

Even as she pushed on his chest, her lower body relaxed against his, her legs opening to accommodate his cock. He needed to taste her. His lips found purchase in the dip where her neck and shoulder met. Kissing her was the sweetest aphrodisiac. She felt the heat, too. He could smell her arousal. She moaned as he sucked, marking her skin. That wanton sound coming from deep in her throat did something to him. For the first time in his life, he lost control. Nothing existed but the exquisite creature in his hold. The hunger consuming him was foreign. The idea was frightening, but more so was letting this moment, this woman, get away. He acted without thinking, sinking his teeth into the welcome softness of her skin to lap up her sweetness. The taste of her blood exploded on his tongue. The effect of it was like a planetary collision. Lust erupted in his veins, setting every cell of his body on fire. His vision went hazy. His erection swelled to the point of pain. His only awareness was the physical need consuming him and demanding more.

Already fiddling with the zipper of her jeans, a faint but unmistakable sound of distress penetrated his dazed senses. Liv was no longer squirming in ecstasy in the death grip of his arms, but in discomfort. When he stalled in alarm, loosening his hold, she used the small hesitation to jerk her head away, causing his sharp teeth to leave two cuts. Drops of blood trickled down into the collar of her shirt.

Zut. By the three moons of Krina, he hadn't meant to do that.

Judging from the size of her eyes and her frantic heart-beat, she was not only hurting, but also frightened.

"Hush, little darling," he said, trying to calm her, but she started fighting him in all earnest.

The drunkard, who was zipping up, turned his head a fraction. Zavir doubted the man would create any trouble, but he couldn't take risks. He couldn't afford complications. He had no choice but to restrain her wrists and held her fast with his body.

"Quiet. He's almost gone."

The man staggered back toward the bar, shooting them nothing but a glazed-over glance. The minute he disappeared around the building, Zavir let go. Liv's small hand shot out. Her palm made a sharp sound as it connected with his cheek. For a moment, they only stared at each other, him trying to get his bearings and she with eyes wide from shock. The sting of her fingers lingered on his skin. As he lifted his fingertips to the burn, her lips parted on a gasp. Fear bled into her pretty eyes.

"You shouldn't have done that," he said.

All that fear morphed into anger. "You shouldn't have bitten me."

No, he shouldn't have, and he already wanted to again. Alarmed by the pull of the idea, he took a step away from her. She brushed her fingers over the wound he'd left and brought them to her face.

Her voice carried a hint of panic. "It's bleeding."

"Calm down. I didn't try to kill you."

Her eyes narrowed on him. "I know what you did."

Had she done it with another Krinar? Suddenly, he couldn't stand the thought. Neither could he help himself from asking, "Talking from experience, honey?"

"Don't forget, I have friends who live with Ks."

His brow lifted at the nickname. He didn't care for it or the wound she covered with her hand.

"I can heal that." He had a nano-healer with him.

"No, thanks."

"Why not?"

"I have my reasons."

If he couldn't take away her discomfort, the least he could do was offer her an apology.

"It doesn't always hurt."

"What?" She stared at him with round eyes. "That's supposed to make me feel better?"

He shrugged. "It's an apology."

"That's your idea of an apology?"

"Take it or leave it."

She gaped. For two of those frantic heartbeats that pulsed in her neck, she seemed to be at a loss for words, and then her jaw locked. Pushing his arm aside, she stomped past him in the direction of the jungle.

"I assume that means our first meeting is over," he said to her back.

She turned on her heel. "You're an asshole."

"Tell me something I don't already know."

"If I didn't need you…" she said through gnashed teeth, letting the rest of her words slide before flinging her frail body once more onto the path that cut into the jungle.

"The marks will vanish," he called after her.

She hurried around the bend in the path, but not before he'd caught a whiff of wet saltiness. Gut softening, his conscience took a knock. Ah, zut. He couldn't stand her tears. It hadn't been his intention to make her cry. He only wanted to lighten the situation with some humor to diminish her stress.

Zut, zut, zut.

She was right. He was an asshole. It was what had

gotten him as far as he'd gotten in the Krinar hierarchy and what kept him alive. Still, he cared as little for the drops of water that spilled from her eyes as for the blood he'd drawn. The female was chiseling at his granite heart, and he didn't like it. It was a weakness, one that could cost his life.

He waited a minute before following in her footsteps to make sure she got home safely. There were many dangers in the jungle, not to mention the men from the bar who could have set a trap up ahead. He'd seen the way they'd salivated over her. Rage tightened his chest at the thought.

His little human was not stupid, though, because she said from the darkness of the jungle, "It won't do you any good to follow me. The information I promised is not at the house where we stay. The Resistance team isn't either."

He wiped another smile from his face. "I'm only seeing you home safely."

"Thank you, but no thanks. I can take care of myself." With a last glare in his general direction, she took off again.

This time, he waited three minutes before following.

Chapter Three

"Where have you been?" Hans exclaimed when Liv entered through the back door.

She jerked. Her spirits sank. She'd hoped they'd be asleep, which at this hour they normally were, but Hans, Erik, and Karl sat around a map spread open on the kitchen table.

"I went for a walk," she said, hoping her voice sounded normal.

Hans' gaze dropped to her neck. "There's blood on your collar."

Shit. She'd flipped up the collar to hide the wound but didn't know blood had stained it.

"It's nothing." She resisted the urge to touch the throbbing mark. "A thorn must've nicked my skin. You know how overgrown the path is."

Turning her back on the men, she lit the gas under the kettle. If she ran off to her room, it would look suspicious.

"What were you doing out on a walk?" Erik asked. He didn't sound pleased.

With a sigh, she faced them again. "I needed some air."

"This is the jungle." Erik gestured around. "Is there anything but air?"

"You know what I mean."

Karl gave her a scrutinizing look. "You shouldn't have gone alone. If you'd told us, one of us would've gone along. It's not safe."

"I'm a big girl."

Erik pushed back his chair. "Liv, you don't–"

"Let her be," Hans said. "We all need a bit of space from time to time."

Shooting him a grateful smile, she said, "Would you like some tea? I'm making."

"Yes," Hans said, "we can all do with a drink. Make it sweet, will you?"

"All right, Hans."

Not able to hold his piercing gaze, she turned back to the counter, busying herself with the preparation of the tea.

"As I said," Karl said, "we'd have to be careful. If we–"

"That's enough for tonight," Hans interjected.

Liv shot him a glance from over her shoulder. It wasn't like Hans to interrupt their work, not when it came to the K attack. Erik and Karl shared her sentiment. They both stared at Hans in surprise as he gathered the map and carefully folded it, making space on the table for the tea.

Forcing herself to behave normally, she carried a tray with mugs to the table and poured the tea. They drank in strained silence, and when Hans called it a night and left, Erik took the mugs to the sink and started rinsing them.

As she reached for a kitchen towel, he said, "Leave it. They can drip-dry." She opened her mouth to protest, but he didn't give her a chance. "We need to practice your defense moves. You're not nearly as good with a knife as you should be."

He was halfway to the basement door when she found her voice. "Why now? It's late."

"We're up, anyway."

"Not tonight, Erik."

He stopped, impatience etched on his face. "We have to be ready, Liv."

She gave an apologetic shrug. "I'm tired."

The truth was, after what happened with the K, her whole body was cold and shaking. She needed time to pull herself together. She needed time to get the information she promised Zavir in exchange for their lives.

"Tired will get you killed," Erik said in a stern voice.

It wasn't that he didn't care. Quite the contrary. He loved her. Survival was everything in their lives. She got that, but she stood her ground, unmoving from her position even as he pointed at the stairs that led to the basement that served as their training room.

"Erik," Karl said softly. "You heard her. Let it go. I'll take care of her training tomorrow."

For a moment, Erik seemed indecisive, but then his features smoothed out. "No more night strolling, Liv. Not alone. If you need air, go for a walk by the river where we have boundary alarms."

"I'm not a child."

"You're our responsibility. I don't need to remind you how dangerous this mission is. People are watching everywhere. Our job is to stay low, not to gallivant around the jungle."

"You want me to be a prisoner here?"

"If you don't act responsibly, you will be."

"You can't be serious."

"That's enough." Karl got to his feet. "We're family.

We have no one but each other." His voice softened as he turned to his sister. "I know you're not a child, Liv, but Erik and I are only trying to protect you. He's right. No more excursions alone. This mission is hard on all of us, but you have to keep the end-goal in sight. Once the Ks come down, we'll have our freedom back. What we're working on is bigger than you or me or this organization. It's not worth compromising for the sake of getting some air. We're all suffering from cabin fever. We just have to deal." Speech done, he nodded. "Go on. Get some rest. I'll meet you at five in the morning for weapon training. Agreed?"

She didn't agree with any of it, but there was no point in arguing. Her older brothers believed with all their hearts in what they were doing. No argument was going to sway them. There was nothing to do but fake acceptance and bid them goodnight.

Once in the tiny room next to the one the three men shared, she lay down on the bed in the dark, listing to the noises they made as they retired for the night. Even with the men right next door, she'd never felt lonelier. They were close, she and her brothers. Hans was their childhood friend. What she was planning ate a hole in her gut, but she saw no other way. She focused on the sounds coming through the thin wall instead, and when she heard three distinct snoring noises, she got up quietly. Avoiding the floorboards that creaked, she sneaked down the hallway and into the basement on bare feet, feeling her way. Once she was inside the room with the door closed behind her, she used the light of her phone to access the safe where Hans kept the USB drive that held the most incriminating information in the world. Only four people knew the code—her, her brothers, and Hans. When they discovered their information had been leaked, her guilt would be obvious, but it wouldn't matter. By then, they'd be safe and far away from here, and five thousand lives in Lenkarda saved.

There was no time to waste. Palms sweating, she extracted the drive and booted up the laptop on Hans' desk. She'd lied to Zavir about where the information was kept. Hans argued their cabin was the perfect hiding place because it was so obvious. No one would think them stupid enough to keep it there. The minutes drew on as the files copied, her heart keeping track of each second as it clicked over. After what felt like forever, the green light pinged. She inserted the empty drive, dragged and dropped the information, and wiped out her traces on Hans' computer, thanks to Karl's training in electronics.

The way back to her room was like walking a minefield. Every creak of the wooden walls made her jump, but it wasn't nearly as gut wrenching as the guilt that burned a hole in her soul.

This was for Erik and Karl.

They'd promised her parents on their deathbed to take care of her, but she'd made a promise, too. She'd vowed to watch out for them and keep her family safe. They were all she had left, and she wasn't going to watch them die in a dead-end mission with a futile purpose.

Back in her room, she hid the drive under the floor-board she'd wiggled loose and got into bed, fully clothed. It was only then, when she grew quiet and her heartbeat stilled, that she became aware of the throbbing in her neck again.

Chapter Four

No information was available on a Resistance cell growing right under their noses, especially since the last Resistance attempt had been squashed with the Keiths still awaiting trial, but the Krinar had their hunches. There had been talk of new attacks, although vague. It couldn't hurt doing a little investigation himself. One should never put all your faith in an informant. It wasn't that Zavir didn't believe the enticing human. It was just his nature to be cautious. Some called it distrustful, but he preferred to call it levelheaded. No informant was one hundred percent loyal, which was why he put out word of a reward being offered for any information pertaining to a Costa Rican Resistance cell. The reward was big enough to make spilling the beans, as the human saying went, well worth the effort.

The informant was everything he hadn't expected. He hadn't had the time to read the file Korum had sent before their meeting. He'd only gotten it an hour before he'd entered the bar, as he'd been wrapping up an ambush. For starters, she was short, even for a human. Delicate. The color of her eyes was most unusual, a violet-blue like the trizni flower on Krina. Most Krinar had dark-colored eyes, and he was still not used to the lighter tones of humans. Her pale skin had glistened with perspiration. A dark braid had fallen over her shoulder, the ends of the silky hair brushing the tip of her breast. Breasts. She had beautiful ones. A woman's ones. The female who had been waiting in the bar for one of the most dangerous men in ten galaxies from here to Krina didn't look like she had many Earth years in age, although her file confirmed she was twenty-five. Indeed, it had seemed impossible that she was his target, but from the way the males had stared, not to mention the filthy bastard who'd had his hands on her, she'd turned into the target of many a man. A young, pretty woman with wide eyes and fretting fingers in a place like that had two things written all over her–innocence and prey. He'd been a step away from taking the man's head off, but she'd surprised him even more with the knife stunt. She had more guts than all the men who'd been in that room put together. Still, she was no match for a pack of human wolves, which is partially why he'd kissed her. Creating an excuse hadn't been the only reason, though. In a non-verbal language all males, regardless from which planet, understood, he'd staked a claim. At least, that had eliminated the dangerous intentions of those wolves who'd practically been drooling over the lamb who'd been so foolish as to enter their lair.

He'd followed the little human to her cabin to make sure she returned safe and established there were three men, assumedly her brothers and the leader. He could've taken the men then and there, but he knew their type. Chances were they wouldn't give up their teammates, not even under torture. The best strategy was to let Liv do the work and bring him the information. In order to complete this mission successfully, he needed to win her trust, not an easy task, seeing they'd gotten off on a rocky start. That rocky start had everything to do with his dick and nothing with his military conditioned brain, but he couldn't be blamed for getting *hot and bothered* around her. With her soft curves and cute freckles, he'd never seen any woman like her. She was different from the tall, slender, toned Krinar women he usually entertained. Frail and vulnerable, she awakened his protective side. For the first time, he understood Korum's reaction in the arena when he'd thought Mia's life had been in danger from Saret. Zavir had helped to protect Mia, but it had only been a job. He hadn't felt the fear for the human woman's life he'd glimpsed in Korum's eyes. He got an inkling of that fear now. Liv was brave, but she was mortal. Her ultra-femininity called to the male inside him while her humanity drew him in the most basic sense of her biological makeup—his lust for her blood. The combination of male protectiveness and lust was what had made him not only kiss her, but also bite her. No, no one could blame him for getting physical. The absurdness of the situation in the bar hadn't escaped him. He'd been sitting there with his dick half exposed and fast growing hard, but what was to be expected when a pretty woman was staring down his pants? She'd flashed him a good view of her cleavage as she'd leaned over the table, which hadn't helped. At the sight of his arousal, her cheeks had glowed like the pinkest love apples on Krina. He'd wanted nothing more than to taste her then and there, which he'd foolishly done, and it was going to happen again. He wasn't in the habit of lying to himself or making promises he couldn't keep. He wanted the informant, maybe too much. The solution to every problem was logic. It was simple. He knew what he had to do. He'd be cured from this persistent hard-on and obsessive thoughts, and the Resistance would come crashing down before harm could be done to the Krinar Center. Two birds with one stone, another favorite human expression of his. Korum wasn't going to like it, but Zavir wouldn't be the first to play dirty.

THE FOLLOWING NIGHT, he scanned the surroundings in advance to ensure there were no threats before waiting at the same table. The female arrived five minutes before the agreed time. The second she stepped over the threshold, his body took notice. His lust combusted like a big bang, instantaneous and loud, the rush of it deafening in his ears. All his intentions of keeping this meeting cool blew up in vain. Dressed in mud-stained jeans and a faded, long-sleeved shirt with heavy-duty boots, he'd never seen anyone more beautiful. Or delicious. The glands under his tongue swelled, bathing his mouth in saliva. He was like a conditioned dog, his tongue dragging on the floor from the mere memory of how she tasted. How was it possible that this meager human could hold such power over him?

Scrutinizing him, she took the chair at the opposite side of the table. He pushed the food he'd ordered toward her. At the sight of the fried chicken, her eyes widened before her expression tightened.

"What?" he said, adopting a tone of mock innocence. "I thought you might be hungry."

"How did you know–?" She bit off the sentence, shaking her head.

"That greasy food is your favorite?" He'd done some investigations that had nothing to do with the Resistance, but she didn't need to know.

"Chicken?" she said, eyeing him with distrust.

"It's a soya substitute, so don't get too excited. It's the best I could do."

"I know how hard it is to come by even the substitute here. Why would you go to so much trouble for me?"

"You need to eat."

"You're trying to make this look like a date, aren't you?"

"There's that, too."

"As long as you remember this is make-belief. No kissing this time."

"What if I asked you on a real date?" He was only half-kidding. "Would you kiss me?"

"I'm not in the habit of kissing men in public."

"A date in private can easily be arranged."

"I'm not meeting with you alone."

She was right not to trust him, but it wasn't going to make much of a difference. He'd always get her alone.

"Eat," he said. "I'm not going to poison my informant."

She glanced at the food again. "I suppose it would be rude to waste it, since you've gone to so much effort."

He couldn't tell if she was being sarcastic or sincere, but he didn't care. As long as she was wolfing down the food like a starved kitten, he could watch her all night.

Nothing was left on the plate when she wiped her mouth on the napkin and downed the glass of sparkling water with a slice of lemon waiting on the side.

"Thank you," she said.

It was the first nice thing she'd said to him, and he liked it, more than he'd ever expected.

"You're welcome, kitten."

"I'm not a kitten."

"You are when your claws come out."

She crossed her arms. "I don't get you."

"What's there not to get?"

"I never know when you're serious."

"I'm always serious."

She sighed before motioning at his empty place setting. "You're not eating?"

"Not what's in here."

"Right." She eyed his body. "Not the greasy type, huh?"

"Nope."

"Well, thank you again for the meal. It's been a while since I ate anything that tasted like fried chicken."

She smiled, and a hundred mega volts of lightning hit his stomach.

Pushing to her feet, she continued, "I better get going soon before my brothers become suspicious."

This time, she took the lead, taking them into the darkness of the jungle that bordered on the bar. She stuck her hand down her bra and pulled out something that she handed him. A computer stick, the old-fashioned kind.

As if reading his mind, she said, "Hans prefers to spend money where it matters, on weapons. We don't have a state-of-the-art IT system."

Their fingers brushed when he took the stick. He dropped it in his pocket. "Do you trust me, Liv?"

Her wide, blue eyes searched his. "Do I have a choice?"

"Not good enough. If we're going to work together, I need to know you're on my side."

Her expression softened, denting the hard armor of his heart. He was a first-class jerk, but she'd learn soon enough he was the devil himself.

"Yes." She blew out a breath. "I trust you. Korum spoke very highly of you."

"Good." Gently, he cupped her cheek. "I'll get you and your brothers out, but if no one is to be hurt, my attack needs to come as a surprise. I can't come in with weapons and blow up the place. If your leader has even an inkling of our plans, I'm a dead man. Do you understand?"

Her eyes grew even bigger as the reality of their somber situation sank in. "You're planning on capturing the entire team alone?"

"This is the safest way to take everyone alive."

"You will let everyone go unharmed, as agreed?"

He dropped his hand to her shoulder. "They will have to be rehabilitated to some extent. You know that."

Biting her lip, she stared into the distance.

"It's better than getting killed, Liv, because that's what'll happen if I don't stop them. That's what would've happened if you hadn't come to me."

She scanned his face. "How will that affect their lives?"

"It's only the Resistance part they won't remember. It'll be as if it never happened. If you want, we can fill the blank with any memory of your choice. They could've come to Costa Rica on holiday or for humanitarian work."

"No," she said quickly. "No false memories. If it has to happen, I don't want more erased than what's absolutely necessary." She wrapped her arms around her body. "Even then, I'll never forgive myself."

"Liv." His grip on her shoulder tightened, drawing her closer. "You know these men better than anyone. You grew up with them. Am I right? They'll never give up, not until they're dead. You said so yourself."

She didn't answer, but he could see the truth in her eyes.

"It's not your fault, kitten. You're doing the right thing."

Her voice came out on a whisper. "Is it safe?"

"You know it is."

Her chest rose with a deep breath. "Fine." She covered

her face with her hands. "Oh, my God. I can't believe I'm making a decision on behalf of others' minds, their very memories, as if bargaining over the price of a loaf of bread."

"Don't. We do what we have to for the ones we love."

"Yes." She gave him a pained look. "For the ones we love."

"That's my girl." His smile was meant to be reassuring, but the tension in her slight body didn't abate.

Pulling her to his chest, his arms went around her as if it was the most natural thing on Earth to do. She rested her head against his chest as if his body was made for her. Their worries, distinct and yet empathetic in the cause that bound them, intertwined. Her heat bled into his cooler skin. In a nanosecond, flames licked over his body. What he promised himself wouldn't happen, did. He lost all reason. He forgot every promise he'd made to himself as he lowered his head to hers, searching for the warmth of her lips. He expected resistance, half hoped for it, because it would've forced him to take a step back and clear his mind, but she not only welcomed him, she met him with her own brand of heat. Her fingers speared through his hair, dragging him closer while she sucked his tongue into her mouth. He groaned into the kiss, letting his hands roam to the curve of her hips, cupping them possessively.

"Zavir," she moaned, jerking the T-shirt from the waistband of his pants. "I want to feel your skin."

"Zut, yes."

Just like that, they were back at square one, with Liv pushed up against the tree. This time, she wrapped her legs around his waist. He rotated his hips, brushing his cock over the apex of her sex to find relief for the unbearable need centered in the lower half of his body, but it only fueled the fire. His desire burned hotter than before. She whimpered, more desperation slipping into their kiss. Supporting her ass with his hands, he ground against her, not only smelling but also feeling the wetness of her arousal through his pants.

"Woman, you drive me mad."

She lifted his T-shirt, exposing his chest, while her other hand fumbled with the button of his waistband. It was as much as he could take. A tearing noise blended with the distant chirping of night insects. Her shirt fell to the ground. He barely suppressed a growl at the sight of her breasts. Full and round, they were covered by a modest white bra. He wanted those curves naked, but her hands were frantic, trying to undo his zipper without success. He only lowered her long enough to push both of their pants over their hips before he bent his knees, positioned his cock, and thrust into her wetness.

A scream tore from her throat. She was wet, but so tight, tighter than he could've imagined. He grimaced with ecstatic pleasure, grinding his teeth and forcing himself to keep still.

"Zavir."

His name sounded too much like a protest, and he when he got his eyes to focus again he was staring at Liv's pale face, streaks of wetness coating her cheeks.

He rested his forehead against hers, his thumbs brushing over her hips. "You're so tight, kitten."

"I can't," she whispered.

"Hush, little darling. Just let me be inside you."

"Zavir, it's—"

She moaned loudly as he slid in another inch. He had no choice but to cover her mouth if they didn't want attention from the bar.

"Shh. I'm going to make this good for you."

She shook her head meekly, as if she disagreed, but

they were too far gone with the head of his cock shoved up her channel and a waterfall of ecstasy promising to crush down on both of them.

"Zavir, please," she mumbled into his hand. "What are we doing? I'm scared."

"You're safe with me."

He held her gaze as his free hand moved between their bodies, reading her reaction as his thumb found her clit. Her eyes rolled back when he gently massaged the nub. More wetness coated his cock. He slipped another inch deeper, her muscles adjusting and letting him in. She panted into his palm, her moans telling him she didn't feel pure pleasure.

"Just a little more," he coaxed. "It'll soon be better."

She shook her head, but only got out another mewl when he claimed one more inch.

Slowly, he took her, until he was halfway home. They had to consummate this. It was a driving act he felt in his bones. The last sprint was going to be the hardest, but after that there'd be release.

"Bite into my hand," he instructed.

She blinked up at him in confusion, but he didn't give her time to contemplate the request. It was either drag out the agony or get it over with so she could find pleasure. With a last thrust, he drove home.

His hand muffled her scream. It wasn't supposed to happen like this, but how could he help it? How could he stop the inevitable?

She whimpered as he started moving, but she wasn't pushing him away. She was clinging to him with both arms and legs.

"That's it, sweetheart. Let me make it better."

He took his time, letting her wetness coat them both before he increased his pace, matching the stroking of her clit to the rhythm. In a short while, her frown smoothed out, and her gasping turned to panting, enough so he could remove his hand from her mouth. He had to be careful of his strength. The force of his desire could easily hurt her. A few more thrusts and she tightened on him, her release drawing her whole body into a violent spasm. Her head fell back against the tree, and her legs were already starting to relax their grip around him. He held her up with one hand, chasing his own release. The pace was fast, the rhythm harsh. One more thrust and he came with a grunt, exploding inside of her. It was the most powerful climax of his life, and he'd had a long life. The only thing dampening his euphoria was that his tantalizing little human had endured more than just pleasure.

"I'm sorry," he murmured, cupping her face and kissing her with as much tenderness as he was capable.

"We didn't use protection."

"Relax. I can't give you babies. Diseases, either."

"I know, but…"

"But what?"

"Nothing." She pushed on his chest. "You better let me down before someone comes."

With regret, he obliged, even though he wanted to keep his cock inside her longer. She was right. Besides, as tight she was, she had to be sore. His regret intensified when she flinched as her feet hit the ground.

"You're hurting," he said.

"I'm fine."

When she reached for her jeans, he stopped her with his fingers locking around her wrist. She shot him a questioning look as he adjusted his pants before taking the nano-healer from his pocket.

"Zavir, what are you doing?"

He showed her the device. "This will take your discomfort away."

"No." Her voice was shaky, but her tone firm. "I know what it is. It'll plant a tracker in me."

"How do you know that?"

"In the Resistance, we have access to certain information."

"Will shining you be a problem? You work for me, now."

"My brothers will know if I've been shined. We have devices at home that scans everyone who crosses the threshold."

He didn't like the idea of letting her go like this, even less that he wouldn't be able to track her. He preferred to keep tabs on her for reasons that went beyond professional, reasons he yet had to reveal to her.

She freed her hand and pulled up her jeans, fastening them with another wince.

"Liv…" he started, for the first time in his long life at a loss for words. "It's not always like this."

"I know." She avoided his eyes. "We got carried away."

He gripped her chin to turn her face back to him. "It's more than that. You can't deny there's chemistry between us."

"Of course." She smiled but looked a little sad. "Chemistry." Escaping the cage of his arms, she pushed away from the tree. "I have to go before someone discovers I'm gone." She picked up the shreds of her shirt. "I'll need to borrow a shirt from somewhere."

"Give it here." Putting the nano-healer away, he took a fabricator from his other pocket and fixed her shirt.

"Wow." She gaped at him. "How does it work?"

"With nanotechnology. It's called a fabricator."

The information was confidential, but it didn't matter that she knew, not any longer.

"Do you just happen to wander around with nano-healers and fabricators in your pockets?"

He helped her into the shirt. "In my line of work, I always need a nano-healer." He started buttoning it up. "I brought the fabricator to create a transport pod for later."

"That little thing can make a pod? What else can you make with it?"

"Nothing too technical. It's not advanced enough to make a ship."

"How did you get here?"

"By pod, but I had to disintegrate it as I couldn't simply park it on the town square. It would've attracted unwanted attention."

"You can make and take things apart with that little device."

"I wouldn't advertise that too broadly. It's information we still keep confidential." Although, he guessed it wouldn't be long before knowledge of the existence of the technology would leak out.

"Does every K have one?"

"No, only the ones who need it for work or the wealthier ones who can afford it."

"What exactly is your designation? I know you're a fighter, like a soldier, but the Ks don't have an army."

He smoothed his palms over her shoulders, adjusting the shirt. "I'm a guardian."

"What do guardians do, except take out Resistance cells?"

"We maintain law and order."

"Are you based at Lenkarda?"

"I'm based wherever I'm needed."

"I see." She fiddled with the shirtsleeves. "I better go. Thanks for repairing my shirt."

His hands tightened on her shoulders. "You don't have to go back to the cabin. I can arrange for you to stay in town while I execute the attack. You can tell your brothers you're going to visit Anita."

"No," she said quickly. "They'll know something is up if I suddenly want to leave. Besides, I don't want to implicate Anita. If my brothers find out she helped me–"

"It won't matter. We're erasing that part of their memories, remember?"

A shadow crossed her face. "How could I forget?"

"Stop blaming yourself for doing the right thing."

She stared up at him, her eyes pleading. "I can't bear for anything to happen to them."

"Trust me. I'm their only chance to make it out of this alive."

Her voice was a whisper. "You're risking your life, aren't you? You're going up against a hundred men or more…"

"I'm not a mere man."

"No, but still. They have weapons."

"I've done this before."

"From what Anita told me, you were very lucky."

Crossing his arms, he grinned. "That's kind of an insult, insinuating I took down armies only because I got lucky." He cocked an eyebrow. "Every time?"

"Fine, you're a good guardian, and you're a K, but you can die."

"Indeed, which is why nothing of my plan can fall on the wrong ears."

"When are you coming for us?"

"Next week, Friday."

"Next week?" she exclaimed.

"The sooner the better. Is that a problem?"

"I just thought…" She worked her bottom lip between her teeth. "I just thought we'd have a bit more time."

"Delaying it isn't going to make it easier."

"I know."

"Hey." He touched her shoulder. "It's going to be all right. I'll get you and your brothers out. Do you trust me?"

For another moment longer, her shoulders remained tense, but then her body slackened. "Yes, I trust you."

"Good." He dropped his hand to feel the outline of the computer drive in his pocket. "Is this all the information?"

"Everything," she agreed with a nod.

"Including the location of the Resistance cell?"

"Here as well as internationally. If you come for them here, the others around the globe will know. You can't be everywhere at the same time."

"No, but with the proof you're giving us, they'll be removed from their positions and taken into custody. We'll keep it quiet until my attack, so your leader doesn't become suspicious. We can't let him know someone is leaking information."

"They'll be charged with treason."

"Each as he or she deserves. We're not on a witch-hunt, Liv. It's my job to wipe out movements that pose a threat to our conjoined safety. It's not my job to roll the people who threaten us in cotton wool and make sure they suffer no inconvenience in jail. I pull out the trouble by the roots. What happens after is the ambassador's job. I'm not here to offer peace negotiations. You knew that when you reached out to me."

"It's just… I feel responsible."

"They'll thank you later for their lives."

A deep sigh escaped her lips.

"Be ready," he said. "Don't do anything, such as

packing a bag, that'll make your team suspicious. Go about your day as usual. I'll take care of the rest."

Her delicate throat moved as she swallowed. "At what time will you attack?"

"When is their guard down the most?"

"At lunchtime. We're short of staff, so there'll be only two men watching the borders. They always rotate positions randomly, so I can't tell you where they'll be."

"Got it. Be ready at lunchtime, then. Where are you normally at that time?"

"I'm helping to serve the food."

"Will your brothers be with you?"

"Yes, and Hans, the leader. They take turns at the medicine depot at that hour."

"Armed?"

"No, but some of the other men will be."

"What's the afternoon routine?"

"After lunch, there's training. Dinner is at six. The men usually hit the sack around eight."

"Make sure you keep your brothers at the depot, and all will be well. You can't share this with anyone, not even the people you love and think you trust. Do you understand?"

She gave a nervous nod. "I do."

"We've taken too much time, already," he said with regret, not ready to leave her. "I'll walk you back."

"No. It's safer if you don't. I'll be fine."

Unable to resist a last touch, he gripped her fingers. "I'll see you soon."

She straightened her back, looking brave and vulnerable at the same time. "I'll be ready."

"Go."

Giving her permission to return to the miserable shack in which she lived went against everything inside him, but he didn't have a choice. She was right. It would raise an alarm if she disappeared or left. Anyway, he'd be following in her tracks, ensuring nothing happened to her on the way.

A few steps away, she glanced back at him from over her shoulder. "Thank you, Zavir, for saving us."

He couldn't even reply to that. He deserved none of her thanks. He only hoped she'd eventually forgive him.

Chapter Five

The K had followed her home again. Liv wasn't stupid. He'd been quiet, but the jungle had been quieter, telling her even the hairy insects and giant bats were aware of the alien's imposing presence. Despite his cocky attitude and scary roughness, it was a sweet gesture, and what had sold her on trusting him. He didn't have to do it. It was gentlemanly behavior and in direct contrast with what they'd done against the tree. Her cheeks flamed in shame. What had she done? What had come over her?

The ache between her legs reminded her exactly of what she'd done. It was nearly impossible to resist the obnoxious K, and she didn't even like him that much. Maybe just a little, when he wasn't sarcastic and rude. When he brought her food that tasted like fried chicken and saw her home safely, it was hard to remember he was a jerk. A jerk who'd had his erection buried in her so deep she still felt it in her womb.

Covering her face with her hands, she took a deep breath. She couldn't let the men see her in this state. They'd immediately know something had happened. She just had to pretend sex with the alien never occurred. She scoffed at herself. Yeah, right. Like the throbbing in her neck didn't return every time she got aroused, which was every time she thought about Zavir.

Stop it, Liv.

The cabin was already in sight. Taking a few drags of the humid night air, she squared her shoulders and opened the door as quietly as she could. She'd oiled the hinges that morning, so it didn't make a squeak as she closed it behind her. Letting out the breath she was holding, she leaned against the door to find her balance. The men had to be sleeping, because the cabin was quiet. She longed for a shower to wash away the remains of sex and soothe the sting between her legs, but there was only the outdoor shower, which made too much noise. She didn't want to risk waking up someone. The bucket of water, washcloth, and bar of soap in her room would have to do.

About to slip to her room, a creaking floorboard drew her attention. A shadow appearing in the doorway that led to the hall made her jump. Karl's features became visible in the moonlight that filtered through the window.

She pressed a palm on her chest. "Oh, my God, Karl. You gave me a fright."

"Get your jacket," he said grimly. "We have to go."

Her heart slammed between her ribs. "Where?"

"The camp. I'll bring the Jeep around."

"The camp? Now? Why? What happened?"

"We'll explain when we're there," he said, already on his way to the door.

"Where are Hans and Erik?"

"They're already there."

His figure disappeared through the doorway. He didn't turn to see if she was following but made straight for the camouflaged awning where they kept the Jeep. Something momentous had to have happened. Maybe there was an attack somewhere, or one of their presidential supporters had pulled out.

Not bothering with a jacket, she locked the door and rushed after him. She was barely seated before he took off with screeching tires. The road was bumpy, and he drove too fast. She had to hold on with both hands to not bump her head on the roof of the vehicle. With the open windows, it was too noisy to interrogate him further. She waited until they parked in a cloud of dust in front of the compound they called the camp. To the left was the bunker where the ninety-something men slept. The open area in the center served as kitchen and dining space. It had long, makeshift tables and a shade awning to protect them from the sun and rain. The jungle was dense enough to hide them from an aerial view. The wooden building on the right, where they held meetings and trained, was a distance away from the others. That was the direction in which Karl headed. Marching out in front of her, he threw open the door and stood aside for her to enter. Expecting to see ten or more of the most senior men at the camp, she stopped in surprise when there were only Hans, Erik, two Resistance fighters who stood a distance aside, and a third man who had his back turned to her. From the dirty vest and torn jeans, she knew he wasn't with the Resistance. Hans was a military man to his bones. He demanded nothing but the cleanest of uniforms ironed to the last crease.

What was going on? She was about to ask when the visitor turned his head to look at her from over his shoulder. Her heart stopped beating. The blood iced over in her veins. It was the oily haired man from the bar.

"Is that her?" Hans asked with a nod in her direction.

The man raised his arm, finger pointing at her. "That's her, all right."

"You sure?" Erik asked, a strange calmness to his voice.

"There's no mistaking her," the man said, "not with that color skin and eyes."

"All right." Hans looked at Erik, a silent command in his gaze. "Thank you."

Erik took a stack of notes from the table, which he handed to the man. "You can go."

The man licked a finger and flicked through the notes, counting them before pocketing the money. With a last sneer in her direction, he disappeared through the door.

Swallowing, she faced Hans. "What's going on?"

"I think you know," he said, taking two steps toward her.

Shit. She'd been found out. That oily bastard had ratted on her. For money. Son of a bitch. She lifted her chin. It was her word against his. "I have no idea what's going on here."

What frightened her most wasn't the fact that Hans stopped so close to her the tips of his boots touched hers, it was how softly Karl closed the door, almost like an apology.

"Karl? Erik?" She looked between her brothers.

"Where were you tonight, Liv?" Hans asked.

"I went for a walk."

He smiled. "Like the other night?"

"Yes, like the other night."

His smile broadened. "No, you didn't. You went to the bar."

Shit, shit. Her heart beat with a furious rhythm.

Erik crossed his arms, disappointment lacing his tone. "What were you doing in the bar?"

"I'll tell you," Hans said, his mocking smile cold now. "You met a K."

She was so fucked. Why the hell did the man have to run his mouth off?

"You'll believe that cockroach over me?" she asked, acting defiantly.

"The whole town is talking about the K in the bar," Erik said. "Did you honestly think a K in the middle of the jungle would go unnoticed? We've known since last week the Ks are sniffing on our trail." Hurt infused his tone. "We just didn't know it was because of you."

"Why, Liv?" Karl asked, his hands spread wide. "Why did you betray us?"

She had to think quickly, but it was hard with the way she was shaking. "Who said I betrayed you?"

"Why else would you meet with a K? That fucker," he pointed at the door through which the man had left, "said you kissed the K." His face drew into a distraught expression. "Tell me it's not true."

"The blood on your collar…" Hans said. "The two little cut marks. The K bit you."

There was no point in bluntly denying it. They already knew too much. She could only hope to sell them a different reason.

"Fine," she said on a huff. "I met a K in town and didn't tell you because I couldn't. I only wanted to know if it was like everyone said, and you would've freaked out."

"What exactly are you saying?" Erik asked, his stance tense. "What was like everyone is saying?"

She shrugged as if she didn't care, but she felt close to vomiting from stress. "If it's true that their bite is pleasurable."

"You let a K bite you on purpose?" Karl asked, his eyes wild and his face red.

"It's no big deal," she said. "Calm the heck down."

"Twice?" Karl exclaimed. "Because we know you met him again. Juan saw you."

Ah, so the oily man had a name. "You paid that bastard for information on your own sister? He's a creep who tried to attack me."

"As it turns out," Hans said, "we're not the only ones dishing out money for information. There's a big reward offered for information on a Resistance cell running in this little ol' town. Isn't that a coincidence? I wonder who's offering it?"

"I told you, I met a K out of curiosity about what the tabloids say. That's it."

Hans' voice softened. "I'm sure it is."

"You believe me?" she asked hopefully.

"Go," Hans said to Karl, motioning with his head toward the door. "It'll be easier."

"I'm sorry, Liv," Karl said, his voice broken. To Hans he said, "Remember your promise." He stormed to the door, yanked it open, and rushed out into the night.

Erik stepped into her line of vision, his face pale and drawn.

"Don't do this, Erik," she pleaded.

"I love you, Liv," he said, "but I told you this was bigger than you or me or our family. If it had been Karl, I would've done the same."

The twins were inseparable. Hearing Erik's confession, that he'd be willing to hand over the one person he loved more than anyone, more than himself, told her there was no way out for her.

With a last look in her direction, Erik, too, walked to the door. When he was gone, Hans flicked his fingers. The two soldiers moved forward, grabbing her arms.

"What are you doing?" she cried, fighting them.

"You can't do this," she yelled as they pushed her down on her knees behind a chair, her chest against the backrest.

"You leave us no damn choice," one of the men gritted out.

They forced her arms around the chair back, so that she was hugging it, while Hans secured her hands and feet.

Cold sweat starting dripping between her shoulder blades. She knew what this meant. She'd seen it before.

"Please," she pleaded with one of the men when he stepped into her line of vision. "Don't do this."

Instead of replying, he turned his face away, but not before she'd glimpsed the pained look on his face.

"Don't," she whispered.

She wish she could confide in them, tell them that she was trying to save them all, but they'd never believe her. Besides, saying so would compromise Zavir. They'd know what he was planning, and they'd set a trap. Zavir would be killed, and it would be her fault. No, she couldn't do that to him, not when he'd vowed to save her brothers and get them all out alive. Not when she still felt him so deep inside her, in parts of her she didn't care to examine.

Hans dismissed the men, and when the door closed once more, he crouched beside her.

"It could've been me, Liv. You could've given me a chance. You know how I feel about you."

She jerked her head up to look at him. There had always been interest from Hans' side, subtle hints, and vague suggestions, but never the fireworks she'd felt in Zavir's arms. No lust, no passion, no desire, just a common goal and a lifelong tie that comes with family friendship and the responsibilities they share.

"Hans," she said through dry lips, "please."

Features hardening, he pushed to his feet. "Why did you meet with a K, Liv?"

"Hans."

She could only appeal to him as a friend, hearing his footsteps as they fell behind her and farther, to the side of the room where they kept the torture instruments. She counted five, six seconds, and then he walked back to her.

This time, her voice shook. "Hans."

He gave her no warning. Fabric tore with a harsh sound as he ripped her shirt from the collar all the way down to expose her back.

Dragging in a breath, she gritted her teeth, already knowing what was coming before a sharp zip slashed through the air and exploded in a line of blinding agony on her back. Her whole body convulsed in pain. A streak of fire burned diagonally across her back. A whip, she registered through the haze of pain. It was hard to focus on anything more than the pain, which was what the instrument was designed to do.

She prided herself too early on not having made a sound. When the second lash fell, a scream tore from her throat. She hugged the chair harder, the wood pressing into her chest. Her knees wobbled. Only the binding around her arms held her upright.

Whoosh.

The ache was searing, agonizing, burning like ten fires. He'd broken her skin. That was the only explanation for the intensity of the pain. The wetness that dribbled down her back confirmed it.

"What were you doing in the bar, Liv?"

Whoosh.

"Hans!" She gasped for breath, barely keeping her head up.

"What were you doing in the bar?"

Whoosh.

51

Her back arched from the excruciating pain. "I met a K!"

"Why did you meet a K?"

"I-I wanted to know what it was like."

Whoosh. Whoosh.

Her head bobbed, and blackness threatened at the edge of her pain. If only the darkness could take her.

"Did you give the K information about us?"

She couldn't tell him that, so she said, "They would've killed us. All of us. The mission was doomed from the start."

"He brainwashed you."

"No! Please, listen to me. I don't want anything to happen to you or my brothers."

"You disappoint me, Liv. I trusted you. You betrayed us."

Whoosh.

God, she was going to pass out. She gritted her teeth so hard, they had to have cracked.

"The Ks are coming for us," Hans said, bitterness lacing his tone. "When?"

She barely had the strength to shake her head.

Whoosh.

The bite went deeper this time. She tried to pull into herself, but the cruel chair held her up as Hans struck repeatedly.

"When, Liv? When are they going to attack?"

She couldn't take more. She'd rather die. She lost track of the count as more lashes rained down on her with the smell of blood thick in the air. She wasn't conscious of screaming, but her voice was hoarse when Hans finally gave her a reprieve.

"When, Liv?"

Friday. It was on the tip of her tongue. Friday was the

magic word that would make the agony stop. Then there was Zavir with his gray-green gaze and strong hands and cocky words. Friday was the word that would get him killed as surely as she was being whipped on her knees. She couldn't do that to him, not when he was risking his life to take them out alive instead of executing them all for plotting to kill many thousands of his kind, including their human charl.

A gush of air left her lips as she gave up, accepting her fate and the pain that came with it. *This was for Erik and Karl.* The last thing that registered in her mind as darkness crept into her vision was Hans' voice when he said, "Fine, Liv. Let unconsciousness take you, but I'll wake you up again sooner than you care for."

Chapter Six

Of course, Zavir didn't tell the beautiful informant the truth. Doing so could not only potentially compromise him should her team members question her, but also her comrades. If they believed they could bring down Lenkarda's protective shield, they were even more ignorant than the worst so-called freedom fighters. They didn't realize how easy it was to take them out. All he had to do was use advanced technology to fabricate an electric field around their compound, and they'd fry to death. If he was to take them alive, he had to catch them unaware, when they least expected it. Which wasn't Friday. No, it was today.

It would be messy. He didn't like it, but for someone who didn't give a damn about honor or deals, he sure didn't want to break the pretty human's heart. Under the brave veneer she kept up, her feelings were tender. Her tears had proven it, as had the way she'd melted in his arms. No, he wasn't noble, and he wasn't going to pretend to be, but if he killed Liv's brothers, she'd never forgive him, and that wouldn't serve his purpose. Korum had convinced the Council to agree to Liv's terms, albeit reluctantly, and only because Zavir had convinced him Liv wouldn't otherwise give up the Resistance cell's secrets.

Leaving the transport pod a safe distance away in a clearing, he continued his approach on foot. It was more discreet with less chance the Resistance's scanners would pick up his aircraft. Checking his weapons, he pulled a protective shield around himself, courtesy of the advanced Krinar technology. The shield enabled him to move undetected, both invisible to the naked eye and infrared.

It was new moon. The night was dark. Since he didn't need the protection of the thick vegetation for camouflage, he took the fastest way to the compound, which was via the road. The hologram in the corner of his night vision device confirmed the information Liv had supplied was accurate. Every landmark he passed corresponded to the map.

A short way from the camp, he stopped. The building where the men were supposed to be sleeping was dark. There was no movement around. The only window from which light shone was the office. A quick heat scan confirmed the number of humans and their positions. A few soldiers guarded the outlook points. The apparatus showed two bodies in the office. The rest were in the sleeping quarters. This was going to be loud. Pulling up the launch sequence on his wristwatch device, he selected the first target before giving the voice command.

"Fire."

Chapter Seven

Icy coldness pulled Liv from the mercy of unconsciousness. She blinked at the sting and gasped for air as another wave hit her in the face. Coughing, she shook the drops from her eyes. Water. Where was she?

"That's my girl. Welcome back, Liv."

Hans.

At the same time, she placed the voice, memories flooded her mind to mix with the excruciating pain as her nerve endings jump-started to life. Her back was on fire. The ache was unbearable.

"When are the Ks coming?" Hans asked, his voice coming from behind her.

It took all her energy to turn her head enough to look over her shoulder. Hans sat on his knees behind her, a knife in his hands. Her feet were bare, her boots lying to one side. He had to have removed them while she was unconscious. A bucket filled to a quarter with water in which ice cubes floated stood next to her shoes, which explained the water in her face.

"Hans," she said through parched lips, despite the fact that her hair, face, and upper body were drenched.

Grabbing her left foot in his hand, he gently caressed the sole. "Last chance, Liv. When are they coming?"

Her shoulders sagged. Hans was relentless. He wasn't going to give up. Neither could she.

"Give him up," he said, as if he could read her mind. "No K is worth your torture. This is hurting me more than you, sweetheart. Tell me what I want to know, and the pain will stop."

It wouldn't. Hans would kill her. He'd have no choice. He'd have to set an example for the men. Her fate would have to be the same as for all traitors in their camp. It would be a public execution, long and agonizing. Death wouldn't come quick or painless. Maybe Karl or Erik would have mercy and put a bullet in her heart. Or not? Maybe their belief in this mission was too strong.

"Liv?" Hans prompted softly, his thumb brushing the sensitive hollow of her foot. "Who is he? Give me a name and date, and we'll bring him down together. We'll have his head. I know he brainwashed you. We'll fix you, I promise. Trust me."

She took a shaky breath. She wouldn't do this to Zavir. Even if Hans killed her, Zavir would come on Friday, take the men prisoner, and set them free when he'd rendered them harmless. She wouldn't be dying for nothing. Yes. She blew out the mental confirmation with a puff of air.

"What was that?" Hans asked.

She could only shake her head. It was best she saved whatever energy she had left for what was coming. She didn't have to wait long. If she'd thought the whip was harsh, it was nothing compared to the knife. The sharp point inserted just below her big toe, burning through her flesh like acid. A scream she couldn't contain broke free, but the sound was feeble. The burn cut across her sole to her little toe. Instead of cutting off her toe like she'd expected, he was making an incision in her foot. God, it hurt. She tried with all her might to move her foot away from the torturous pain, but Hans' hold was too strong. Her leg shook in his grip.

Another cut.

Another scream.

Over and over.

Pinching her eyes shut, she forced herself not to look, but she could feel the blood trickling down her heel. Her body started quaking all over as it went into shock.

"Liv," Hans said on a groan. "Give me something. Make it stop."

She gnashed her teeth, scraping together the little she had left of her physical force to face him squarely from over her shoulder. "Sorry, Hans. I'm not letting my brothers die." Her voice was unsteady but her words strong. "Give it your best shot."

"All right," he said solemnly, pushing to his feet. "As you wish."

Her heart sank as he went for the pliers. Teeth or nails? Which would it be?

Please, let me be strong. No, let me die now.

There was no such luck for her. Placing the pliers in her line of vision, Hans walked to the corner where they kept the cleaning utensils and returned with the iron.

No, not that. Not the iron. She whimpered as he plugged it into the wall to heat. Pride deserted her. Shamelessly, she called for her brothers, even if they probably couldn't hear her. They wouldn't have stayed in earshot, not for this. Had they agreed with Hans' methods of making her talk?

"Do Erik and Karl know what you're doing?" she asked in a cracked voice.

"I promised them I wouldn't hurt you, that I'd just scare you a bit, but you and I both know you're too strong to be scared. You left me no choice. Talk now, and all this will be over."

She shook her head. "Karl, Erik, they'll never forgive you."

"I don't need their forgiveness. I need to know what you're scheming with the Ks."

Hans returned for the pliers. He drew the cold metal over her shoulder, watching her with a sad look as he made sure she registered the new instrument of torture.

His tone carried regret when he said, "Stick out your tongue."

His intention had barely registered when a bright light penetrated the room. Blinded, she squeezed her eyes shut. A split-second later, the room shook with an explosion. Glass rained down on them as the windows shattered. Her ears rang from the noise. She forced her eyes open. What should've been flames and debris were ripples of thick air, like waves of energy. They rocked her body and splintered the wood of the chair. As the backrest broke into pieces, she fell facedown, her hands and feet still tied. Her brain was going to combust. The white light kept on expanding, pulling her body tight with spasms and making it impossible to think.

"Liv!"

Hans crawled to her on his hands and knees, but the next explosion leveled him with the ground. He curled into a ball next to her, covering his ears with his hands.

They were under attack. It didn't make sense. It wasn't Friday. It couldn't be Zavir. They had to get away.

"Cut me loose," she shouted over the noise, but no reaction came from Hans.

It took enormous effort to get onto her knees, using her bound hands to push herself up. Adrenalin gave her the energy she needed to straighten. There was no time to try and cut herself loose. She needed to get to Erik and Karl. She hopped to the door over shards of glass. The sharp pieces cut her injured as well as her good foot, but she no longer registered the pain. There was only survival instinct. When she threw open the door, pandemonium met her. There was chaos everywhere. Men forced themselves from windows and doors, falling on top of each other. They writhed where they fell, holding their heads between their hands.

"Erik!"

She started hopping in the direction of the sleeping quarters. Where was she even supposed to look?

"Karl!"

The bawling of the men as well as the ringing sound that wasn't only in her ears washed out her calls. Halfway across the yard, she spotted Erik. He was hunched over an automatic rifle, half running, half stumbling in the direction of the office.

"Erik!"

He didn't hear her. He kept on fighting his way through the ripples of air as one would tread against a strong current of water. About to yell again, she bit off the sound as an unnaturally tall man appeared on the perimeter of the light. He stood out not only because he was so big, but also because he moved effortlessly in the midst of the destruction. Her gaze slipped from the ease of his gait to his face, and then she froze.

Zavir.

Impossible.

But there he was.

A different kind of pain lodged in her chest. He'd lied to her. The truth of the realization hurt more than a thousand cuts on the sole of her foot.

Agile and fast, he moved like a predator, a weapon in his hand. As he reached the first man writhing on the ground, he aimed the gun.

The word left her lips before she could stop it. "No!"

Nothing more than a blue zap released from the gun, rendering the man motionless. A stun gun. At the sound of her voice, Zavir looked up, his gray eyes so dark they looked like onyx, and his stance like a tiger ready to pounce. His eyes focused on her. When recognition set in, what she saw in those strange, glowing depths frightened her more than any torture. Time seemed to pause as they stared at each other–her, Zavir, and Erik–each registering shock, and then everything happened at once.

Erik lifted the rifle.

"Erik, no!"

A shot rang out before she'd formulated the last word. Zavir glanced at his shoulder where a red stain was growing on his T-shirt. Erik lifted the rifle again, but Zavir had his own weapon trained, and it wasn't the stun gun. This time, there was no zap.

Her protesting scream fell on deaf ears. Erik fell to his knees, the fabric of his combat pants flowering like red petals on his thigh.

"No!"

She hopped toward where Erik had fallen, but a strong arm clamped around her waist, lifting her off her feet.

"Let me go!" She kicked and fought as much as her constraints allowed.

"Let her go, asshole," a familiar voice said behind them.

No, no. No. Not Karl, too.

Zavir twirled around, his weapon aimed in the direction of the new threat.

"Don't hurt–" she started, but Karl's rifle fell from his hands as he dropped to his knees.

"Oh, my God! You shot them! No! Karl? Erik!"

Repeatedly, she yelled their names, but neither of her brothers moved.

Zavir had lied to her.

He'd broken his promise.

Chapter Eight

The persistent beep of the communication device made Zavir growl. Not now. He was lying next to his little informant, watching her sleeping form. She was peaceful, no longer in pain. The memory of the state of her body, battered and bloodied, ignited fresh rage. He should've killed those damn brothers and tortured the leader. They didn't deserve her. If it weren't for the affection she harbored for them, he wouldn't have given it another thought. To have gone through what she'd suffered, that affection had to go deep.

Another beep, and he couldn't ignore it any longer. Gritting his teeth, he got to his feet and covered Liv's body with a sheet before exiting the room to talk without disturbing her. He gave the voice command and a holographic image flickered to life. It was Korum.

"How is she doing?"

He bit out the words. "Fine, considering."

"We need to debrief."

"Not now. She may wake up at any moment."

Korum's expression hardened. "It wasn't a request."

"The human–"

"The human is part of the debriefing."

He didn't like the way Korum said it. Not one bit.

"I'm waiting for you in the meeting room."

The hologram disintegrated.

An unwelcome foreboding nestled in his stomach, one he couldn't ignore. With another glance at the sealed entrance to the bedroom where Liv was sleeping, he stomped through the quarters to the main exit, commanding it to open and seal behind him. The grounds were big, but it took him only minutes to make it by pod to the big room in the center of the settlement.

Korum waited alone for him, another bad sign. The leader's back was turned to the entrance. He was staring at something that played out on a hologram. Coming to a stop a step behind, Zavir took in the scene. Liv's brothers were being treated for their wounds with nano-healers. In a separate vision, the rest of the cronies were already under-going the rehabilitation procedure.

"Congratulations," Korum said without turning. "You did well."

He was in no mood to be congratulated, not with what Liv had endured and his thoughts being with her instead of the mission.

Korum faced him slowly. "We announced the arrest of the rest of the Resistance world-wide. It made headline news."

"I've seen."

Korum chuckled. "You're fast becoming a legend. The Council will be pleased. They're looking for a new Protec-tor. This will count considerably in your favor."

"Good." Ambition was the last thing on his mind, right now. "How are the Earthlings taking it?"

"The fact that there was no casualties made it easier to

go down. Their ambassadors are reporting it as positive token of our goodwill and desire to live in peace."

His voice came out harsh. "They deserved worse than death."

Korum seemed to understand the underlying reason for his suppressed rage, because he asked, "How is the girl?"

"She's good. Physically, at least."

"Ellet wants to see her."

"There's nothing more the doctor can do for her. I healed her wounds."

"You don't understand. It's not just about checking her physical health."

"Then what?" he said, a tad bit too aggressive.

"The ambassador to Earth wants a report from a medical professional."

"What's his interest in her?"

Korum gave him a level look. "What is yours, Zavir?"

"What do you mean?"

"You can't keep her locked up. She's a free person. The South African ambassador is concerned about her safety. She's part of the Resistance. She needs to be rehabilitated and released like the rest of the group."

His anger flared. "She gave us the information. She doesn't believe in the Resistance."

"That's what she says."

"That's why Ellet wants her. They want to probe her brain."

Korum shrugged. "Standard procedure."

"No."

"No?" Korum seemed amused. "You're assuming I'm *asking* again."

"No one is touching her except me."

"That's not for you to decide. She's not a prisoner of

war. You have to hand the woman over to be checked by our doctors before we return her to her people. I know she helped you, and you're uncharacteristically grateful to her, but you have no basis on which to keep her here."

He steeled his voice. "Yes, I do."

Korum raised a brow. "What may that be?"

"I'm claiming her as charl."

Chapter Nine

With a contented sigh, Liv stretched. Succumbing to the luxurious feeling of waking fully restored, she took another moment to enjoy the soft comfort of the bed and the perfect temperature of the room. Then her eyes flew wide open. It was all wrong. It should've been a scratchy sheet on a hollow mattress in a room feeling like an oven in the tropical climate. Her body should ache from training, her muscles in a permanent state of soreness. The alarm should've rung, too early. She should've been groggy and blurry-eyed from too little sleep.

She went rigid as memories flooded her mind. The attack. Erik. Karl. Zavir had shot them. He'd taken her, and then everything had gone black. The torture. She blinked. She was lying on her stomach, a sheet as cool and smooth as water covering her. Underneath, she was naked. Turning on her back, she took in her surroundings. She'd seen simulations of Krinar dwellings during her Resistance training enough times to know where she was. The walls were off-white and the domed ceiling transparent, like a huge skylight. Through it, she could see the cloudless sky.

Sitting up, she lifted her feet and looked over her shoulder at her back. No wounds. Not as much as a scratch. Even the persistent throbbing in her neck where Zavir had bitten her was gone. So was the ache between her legs. As she glanced down, her cheeks heated at the thought that someone's hands had been there, inside her. All traces of sex were washed away. Her skin looked silky and blemish-free. Someone had cleaned and treated her with a nano-healer. *Shit.* She'd probably been shined, not that she wasn't thankful for the absence of pain.

Glancing around the room, she saw no clothes. There was no furniture but the bed she'd been sleeping in. Even now, the mattress adjusted under her backside, molding into a comfortable cushion that somehow took the strain of sitting upright off her back. Getting to her feet, she looked for cameras or some sort of communication device, but there was nothing. She tied the sheet around her body and inspected the room. She felt remarkably well, better than she'd felt in years, but it was only physically. Inside, she was frantic. Where were Erik and Karl? Were they alive? If Zavir had lied about the day of the attack, he could've lied about keeping the Resistance soldiers safe, too. She didn't worry about Zavir's injury. She'd witnessed how his wounds healed themselves. No doubt he was already back to normal.

There was no point in looking for an exit. The only way she was getting out was if a K released her. There was nothing to do but wait. Her rested state made her sharply aware of how hungry and thirsty she was. The usual aches and pains that came with combat training, as well as the hardness of the life she'd endured for the last few months, masked other, minor discomforts such as a need for water and food.

She'd just sat down on the bed again when an

opening appeared in the wall. Relief and anger washed simultaneously through her as a tall, broad-shouldered, perfectly handsome, and dangerous-looking K walked through it.

Zavir.

He was hands down the most frightening and attractive man she'd ever met, but anger overrode every other emotion.

"You bastard." She jumped to her feet. "You lied to me."

He gave her a closed-lipped smile. "Glad to see you're feeling better."

She charged at him, forgetting for a moment he wasn't a human man she could bring down with her fast fists and martial art skills. He easily caught her wrists before she could plant them in his stomach.

"Where are they?" She jerked her arms, trying to free them. "What have you done to them?"

"If you're referring to your brothers, they've been healed."

She calmed slightly at that. "You shot them."

His onyx-colored eyes cooled several degrees, sending a chill down her spine. "They deserved much worse for what they did to you."

"You said you wouldn't hurt them."

"Even though they were going to kill me, I made sure I inflicted only flesh wounds to immobilize them."

She pulled again, and that time he let her go. "Where are they?"

"In aftercare. They'll be free to go tomorrow."

Her shoulders sagged in relief. "I want to see them."

"In time." His eyes trailed over her. "How are you feeling?"

"Better than ever. Did you…? Was it you…?"

"Yes." His voice was strained. "I administered the treatment."

Her gaze slipped to his shoulder. "Your wound?"

"Has healed, thanks to the nanocytes in my body." His smile turned cocky. "Thanks for your concern."

"I'm grateful you healed me," she replied softly, "but you still lied to me."

"I had to. It was in your best interest."

Her anger escalated again. "I got tortured, believing I was protecting you. I trusted you." That hurt the worst. "I held back telling. I took…" She couldn't even say it. "I took the terrible things Hans did to me to protect you."

"I know what you took," he said quietly. "I'm sorry for what you suffered. If I hadn't given you my word, I would've tortured your leader to death myself."

She wrapped her arms around her body. "Where is he?"

"At the Neuroscience Center, awaiting rehabilitation."

"They're not…?"

"No," he said tightly, "they're not torturing him. They don't need to."

"They're extracting the information about the Resistance from his brain, aren't they?" When he didn't reply, she asked, "When are you letting him go?"

"Tomorrow, with the others."

"Then I'm going tomorrow, too?"

Instead of answering, he turned for the exit. "You must be hungry. You've been out cold for almost twenty hours."

She followed him into a bigger area that, according to the strange, floating furniture, served as lounge, dining room, and kitchen. From what Anita had described to her, it was a smaller unit than the one in which Anita lived. Maybe it was guest quarters.

"Where are we?" she asked as he stepped into the kitchen part of the room. "Lenkarda?"

"Yes."

He rambled off some voice commands, at which dishes miraculously started appearing. She'd had a few picnic lunches with Anita on the beach, but the table had already been set with some of the exotic foods from Krina when she'd arrived. Seeing it being done made her gape as the hovering tabletop quickly filled up with colorful, strange-looking dishes and pitchers of purple juice. No ice.

"Sit," he said, pointing at a side of the tabletop.

She looked around for a chair, and sure enough, a plank came floating toward her to fit underneath her and mold around her back. A pleasant sensation travelled through her body as the carpet not only cushioned but also gently massaged her feet.

"I'm serious, Zavir. I need to see my brothers."

"I said soon. You need to eat." He lifted a brow in challenge. "You want me to feed you?"

"No, thanks." Pulling one of the dishes toward her, she sniffed the red concoction. "What is it?"

"Taste it. It's not fried chicken, but I'm sure you'll like it."

She used a tong-like utensil to serve a portion on her plate. Taking a small bite, she took her time to savor the taste. A mixture of sweet and tangy exploded on her tongue. Nothing compared to it. The closest she could come to a description was tangerine mixed with raspberry, but it didn't do the food justice.

"Good?" he said with a grin as she stuffed the rest in her mouth.

"It's not fried chicken," she said with a full mouth, unwilling to give him any satisfaction.

She was hungrier than she ever recalled. A lack of

good food and eating for the sole purpose of filling up her stomach with dry bread dunked in black coffee like the rest of the soldiers had over the months squashed her appetite, but it seemed to be back with a vengeance. Did it have something to do with the nano-healing? Maybe it had restored her metabolism.

She tried a green dish. It had a meaty taste, the cubes melting on her tongue. She caught herself just in time to keep from humming her approval. Zavir filled a glass with the purple liquid and pushed it toward her.

"Thank you." She took a sip and then gulped down the lot. Delicious. "You were saying about when I was leaving?"

Something in the way he stood there, arms crossed over his chest, watching her, made her put down the glass.

"Zavir?"

He walked around the table and stopped next to her. Cupping her cheek with a broad palm, he looked at her tenderly, as if to soften a blow. "You're not leaving, Liv."

Chapter Ten

"What?" Liv reeled from his touch. "What do you mean I'm not leaving?"

He dropped his hand, his cool demeanor back in place. "You're staying."

The food turned sour in her stomach. Bile pushed up in her throat. "I don't understand. Am I a prisoner?"

His disturbing eyes glittered like cold gemstones. "It depends on how you look at it."

She pushed away from the table, struggling to get up from the plank. "You can't do that. You can't keep me against my will."

"Yes." His voice was sure, strong, apologetic, almost. "I can."

"I gave you what you wanted," she cried out, taking a step away from him.

"Not everything," he said quietly, the dark intent in his eyes frightening.

"They won't allow it. The government will demand my release. I have rights."

"There's nothing your government can do. Accept it, Liv. It'll be easier if you don't fight it."

"Fight what?" she cried out, close to hysteria now. "What the hell am I? A hostage?"

"My charl."

She gasped, taking another step back and almost stumbling when she stepped on the sheet. He gripped her shoulders, straightening her, but she jerked away.

"Your what? No. No, no." She shook her head. "Never."

The tenderness from earlier disappeared, making place for a hardness that settled around his mouth. "There are worse things you could be."

"I don't consent!"

He advanced on her, stopping so close she had to crane her neck to look up at him.

"I don't need your consent."

Her mouth opened in shock, but not a word came out. She was incapable of making a sound.

"I'm sorry if the idea doesn't appeal," he said icily. "I'm sure it'll grow on you."

"Why?" she whispered when she'd found her voice again.

Instead of answering, he simply stared at her. Slowly, the realization hit home. Her skin turned cold and damp, as if she was going to be sick.

"Oh, my God," she said on a whisper. "You planned it. You planned it all along."

He didn't even bother denying the statement. "Information wasn't the only prize I was after."

"Since when?" she said, the delicious food stuck in her throat. He reached for her again, but she pushed him away, slamming her palms on his chest. "Tell me, damn you. Since when did you decide, you were taking me?"

"Since the beginning."

The hysteric feeling threatened to escape. "Since the day we met?"

"Yes."

"Why me?" was all she could get out.

He considered her for a moment, his superior, cruel eyes playing over her face. "We have chemistry."

"You're out of your mind. Chemistry isn't enough for a lifelong commitment."

"There are other things."

"Such as?"

"You're pretty, and you amuse me."

"I amuse you?" she cried in indignation, hurt blooming in her chest. "Like a pet? Like a monkey?"

"Like a kitten."

Tears sprang to her eyes. She hated herself for it more than she hated him. "Fuck you."

"Better watch that mouth, *kitten*. There are consequences for bad behavior."

"Yeah?" She hated the tears that spilled over, demonstrating her weakness. She cringed in shame even as her chest heated in anger. "Even better, go fuck yourself."

"Actually, more like a cub than a kitten." His smile was evil. "Yes, I'd say *even better*. That feral fight in you really turns me on."

"You…" She couldn't think of a worse enough insult. "You're despicable. Dishonorable. We made a deal."

"Sorry, darling. I don't make deals."

"You deceived me. You lied to me!"

"I've done worse."

"You're a…a devil."

"Then I guess you made a deal with the devil." His tone was cold. "Make yourself comfortable. It's going to be a long stay."

Without another word or glance, he stalked toward the wall. It disintegrated, and then he was gone. The wall formed back in place, locking her into her prison.

Chapter Eleven

"You don't look like a man who's just taken a charl," a female voice said behind Zavir.

He turned from the garden where he'd been observing charl strolling through the greenery, some with their cheren, and others together in small groups. Xita, his childhood friend, leaned against a gazebo pillar, observing him with a smile.

"Keep your comments to yourself," he growled. "I need none."

"Nope." She straightened and sauntered his way. "You definitely don't sound like a man on honeymoon."

"Who said anything about a honeymoon?"

"Isn't that what taking a charl is supposed to be like? At least, that's what the other cheren say."

"Exceptional circumstances," he mumbled.

"Yes, I heard."

"Heard what?"

"You took a female against her will."

He scoffed, turning his back on her again. "I'm not the first, and I have my reasons."

"Your libido?" She stopped next to him, nudging his shoulder. "If I recall correctly, it's quite high, but it's been a while. Maybe it's changed."

"What do you want, Xita?"

"I'm just passing through. When I heard you were here, I thought I'd look you up. I thought maybe we could catch up."

"Not this time."

"Ah. So, the libido is waning."

"There's nothing wrong with my libido." There was only one reason Xita would be here. "You're doing the rehabilitation on the Resistance fighters."

"With Saret out of the picture after his arrest, is there anyone better for the job?"

"Word is Haron is taking over Saret's lab."

"Haron's not here yet, is he? Besides, everyone knows I'm the best. That's why the Council sent for me."

Her cocky attitude, which he'd always liked up to now, suddenly irritated him. "How are the twins?"

"Good. When I'm done, there won't be a resisting cell left in their bodies."

His body tensed involuntarily at the next question. "How about their leader?"

"Hans? I'm doing a pretty good job on him, even if I have to say so myself."

"What have you found?"

"You know I'm not at liberty to discuss that. All information is encrypted and going directly to the Council with a big, fat confidential stamp on it."

He scoffed again. "You watch too many human television series."

"What can I say?" Her smile was sultry. "I like to be entertained."

He chose to ignore the suggestive remark. "Then all is set for letting the rebels go tomorrow."

"You don't sound pleased."

He clenched his fists. "If I had my way, they wouldn't be going anywhere other than the graveyard."

"That's a bit harsh, seeing that they haven't actually executed any attacks."

"That's not the point. It's what they planned. It's what they did to Liv."

"Wow."

"What?"

"If I didn't know better, I'd say you feel something for the weak Earthling."

"Liv is anything but weak, and yes, there's chemistry between the *Earthling* and me."

"It's not going to work, Zavir."

"One, I didn't ask for your opinion, and two, you're a scientist, not a relationship expert."

"You should undo your claim on her and set the girl free. It's not too late. You haven't yet given her the nanocytes that will make her immortal."

His back turned stiff. The mere mention of letting Liv go had him tenser than at the verge of an ambush. "Why would I do that?"

"Because to keep a charl, you have to care for someone other than yourself."

He smiled but put no warmth in the gesture. "I like you better when you're full of flattery."

"I'm talking to you as a friend."

He lifted a brow. "As they say on Earth, with you as a friend, who needs enemies?"

She brushed it off with a shrug. "Never heard the expression."

"Anyway, it's too late. I've already given her nanocytes to heal, enough to make her immortal."

"Without the Council's permission?"

"There was no time to consult the Council. She was injured. What difference does it make if I did it before or after I declared I was taking her as charl? In the end, they would've agreed."

"I bet the only reason you didn't get into serious trouble for that is because Korum put in a good word for you." She almost sounded bitter. "Am I right?"

"There's also the part about the Council being grateful the Resistance cell was brought down without any loss of lives."

"Mm, arrogant, as always, I see." Crossing her arms, she stared at the garden. "Are you bringing the girl to the lab?"

"Her name is Liv and no."

"Why not?"

His temper flared. "I already told Korum, I won't submit her to testing or brain probing."

"I meant to see her family."

He made a conscious effort to calm himself. "How did they respond to the procedure?"

"Leaving a portion of their memories blank would've been too traumatic. I had to fill it with something."

"What are you replacing their memories with?"

"The easiest was a holiday."

"I don't want her to see them. I can't face them. The risk that I'll break their necks is too big."

"You have to let her see with her own eyes that they are well. It's in her best interest."

"You mean in your best interest for her to cooperate, should you want to run tests?"

"There's that, too."

"No. No tests."

"Fine. I can't force you to bring in your charl, but if you want her to trust you, you have to keep your promises."

"How do you know what promises I made?"

Tilting her head, she gave him a quiet smile.

"We've been watched."

"My apology, but it was necessary."

He clenched his teeth.

"Bring her around tonight and no more watching. I promise."

"Why are you so keen on seeing this meeting happen?"

"I'm just curious about how her brothers will react upon seeing her. It will be a good test."

"You don't need tests. The method is fail-proof."

"We always need more tests." She blew him a kiss. "I'll see you and your little charl tonight."

Watching her walk away with a sway to her hips, he couldn't help the renewed anger festering in his chest. No one touched Liv. Not without his permission.

———

THERE WASN'T anything to do but pace the room. The apartment had cleaned itself after Zavir had left, and despite her numerous tries, it didn't respond to her requests as it had responded to Zavir's command for food. The entrance to the bedroom was sealed, and she was stuck in the living area, desperate for the bathroom.

After what seemed like hours, Zavir returned. She both dreaded and was relieved at his return. Stepping into the room, his gaze fell on her where she stayed at the far end. How was it possible that those slate-gray eyes both sparked and seemed so flat at the same time? She couldn't place the look he gave her. He seemed perfectly indifferent, which only made her want to behave childishly, preferably by throwing something at him. Fortunately—for both of them—there was nothing in the ivory-colored room she could aim at his head.

Ignoring her, he walked to the bedroom. The wall disintegrated as he approached.

"Zavir?" she said, opting for politeness. Irrational spitefulness wasn't going to help her situation.

He paused to look at her.

"I need to use the bathroom."

His eyes ran over her sheet-clad body.

"If you're planning on keeping me here," she said, throwing out bait for a fight despite her resolution to aim for civility, "you'll have to give me access to at least the basic facilities."

Instead of reacting on the accusation, he simply said, "Consider it done."

She managed a defeated, "Thank you." What else was there to say?

A sliver of warmth heated his eyes. "You're welcome." Turning abruptly, he entered the bedroom. "Come, Liv," he said when she didn't follow.

Like a dog. No, wait, a kitten. If she had a tail, he probably would've expected her to wag it. Keeping her thoughts to herself, she obeyed grudgingly. Two walls had disintegrated, giving access to a bath and dressing room.

"You'll find everything you need in the cleaning room," he said. "I'll be back for you in an hour. Be ready."

She clutched the sheet to her chest. "Ready for what?"

His eyes darkened. "For seeing your brothers."

"Really?" She could barely contain her relief. "You'll let me speak to them?"

His answer was curt. "Yes." He motioned at the shower. "I presume you can figure out how this works?"

"Yes." She definitely didn't want a demonstration.

"If you need anything, say my name, and the house will contact me."

No way. She wasn't calling his name, not even if she was as desperate as she was now for the bathroom.

When she didn't answer, he gripped her chin. "Say yes so I know you understand."

"May I please use the bathroom now?" She couldn't resist a jibe. "Unless you want me to soil your fancy toe-massaging carpet like a naughty pet. I guess I haven't been housetrained yet, huh?"

At the last part, the earlier warmth evaporated from his eyes, leaving them colder than a dark moon on a frosty winter night. "Careful, kitten. I'll only let you push me so far."

She jerked her face from his hold, hurrying to the bathroom before she could say something that would really get her into trouble. How she hated the big, arrogant K. She longed for a door to slam, but there was only the sleek opening of the wall and silence as it closed behind her.

She took a moment to freshen up, but also to gather her composure. Losing her cool wasn't going to get her out of here. Neither was aggravating Zavir.

When she was done, she tested her newly lifted restrictions by ordering the room to open. This time, the house obliged. A quick walk-through told her Zavir had left, again. Dropping the sheet, she went to the dressing room and selected one of the many pastel-colored dresses and a matching set of underwear. It had been ages since she'd worn a skirt, and she enjoyed the feel of the soft fabric around her thighs. She did nothing else to improve her appearance, as Erik and Karl were used to her in mud-stained clothes and her hair pulled back in a ponytail. She couldn't help but notice how silky her hair felt and how it fell down her back in a straight curtain, all the kinks and frizz gone.

The wait was excruciating. To pass the time, she sat down on a plank and asked for something to read. The house responded by sending a tablet her way. She snatched it from the air, half worried it may disappear again. She wasn't sure if Zavir intended for her to have permission for anything other than the bathroom and food. She was, after all, his prisoner. Checking the library list on the tablet, her mouth dropped open. All her favorite books were included, even the ones she'd always wanted to read but had never gotten around to. How did Zavir–? No, she didn't want to know. Maybe it was the house. Maybe it had access to her thoughts.

She was halfway into the first chapter of a memoir when Zavir returned.

Approval marked his tone. "I see you're settling in."

"Keeping busy," she corrected.

He held out his hand. "Let's go."

She got to her feet but ignored his proffered hand. "I can walk by myself."

"It's for your protection," he said patiently.

"My protection?"

"Many Krinar are unhappy that you've not been rehabilitated."

"Do you mean I'm not safe?"

"As my charl, no one may touch you, but it doesn't mean someone won't try."

Her insides shook a little at the knowledge. Great. As if her life couldn't get more complicated.

He kept his hand extended. "Take it or leave it. Of

course, if you don't want to see your brothers, we can stay home."

"It's not home."

"My patience is running low, Liv. You have two seconds to decide."

At that, she reluctantly slipped her hand in his. His fingers closed around hers–firmly, but not too tight.

A pod waited in front of the dwelling. She'd never been in one and couldn't help a case of nerves as a floating seat shifted beneath her, and Zavir took off, heading south. The floor was transparent, allowing her a view of the jungle and isolated, oblong buildings below. Thanks to the map Hans had had of the Center, she could orientate herself. They were heading toward the medical center.

They landed and entered the off-white building. Sunlight filtered through the walls that were transparent from the inside. The Krinar they passed stared at her, some expressionless, and others openly hostile. She couldn't blame them. She had been with the Resistance, after all. She felt increasingly ill at ease. When they finally entered the restricted area, she blew out a strained breath. At least she was hidden from the curious eyes. In here, the medical personnel only regarded her with clinical interest.

Zavir squeezed her fingers. They'd stopped in front of a digital number on a wall. "Ready?"

How could he even ask? "Of course."

Her heart flapped wildly in her chest as he uttered a command for the access to open. Stepping over the threshold, she took in the room. Karl was sitting on a plank next to a hovering surface, facing a female Krinar with striking features. The woman got to her feet when they entered.

"You must be, Liv. I'm Xita."

Zavir's hand tightened around hers to the point of pain.

For a moment, he held her back, as if he wouldn't let her go, but when Xita shot him a look, he lifted his fingers one by one. Liv rushed to Karl, putting her arms around him.

He uttered an awkward laugh. "Hey. What's going on?"

She blinked back tears. "I'm just so happy to see you."

He seemed confused. "We only saw each other yesterday."

She glanced at Xita, not sure how to respond.

Xita placed a hand on Karl's shoulder. "We were just chatting about your holiday. Karl told me how much fun you're having. Come on, Zavir." She came around the table. "Let's give them some privacy."

Zavir didn't budge. He crossed his arms over his chest and widened his stance. "I'll stay."

Xita looked exasperated, but she didn't challenge him. "Nice meeting you, Liv. I hope we'll meet again soon."

When she was gone, a plank drifted closer to accommodate Liv.

"How are you?" she asked, sitting down next to Karl.

"I'm well," Karl answered without hesitation. "Exceptionally so. How's the honeymoon?" He grinned at Zavir.

Liv blinked at him. "What?"

"The honeymoon," he said, frowning. "That's the reason we came here on holiday, to celebrate your engagement. You are still moving in together, aren't you?"

The blood drained from her body, leaving her dizzy. She looked at Zavir, unspoken questions on her mind, but his face was expressionless.

"It's good," she replied softly. "The holiday is really good."

Karl patted her hand. "I'm happy for you. You deserve it."

She held Zavir's gaze. "Do I?"

"Of course." Karl turned to Zavir. "Thanks for organizing accommodation for us here. That was thoughtful, although a hotel would've been fine."

Zavir's smile looked more like a grimace. "Don't mention it."

"Do you need anything?" Liv asked, watching her brother closely.

"No, but thanks. Our accommodation is top. I'd like to go back to the beach tomorrow with Erik. Maybe you'd like to join us?"

"We'll think about it," Zavir said.

"What did you do at the beach?" Liv probed gently.

For a moment, Karl seemed confused. "We swam."

Liv glanced at Zavir, concern clouding her earlier relief. "With Erik?"

"Yes, Erik was there." He frowned.

"Is something wrong?" she asked.

Karl touched the side of his head. "I had to tell you something, something important, but I forgot."

"It's okay," she said quickly. "You'll remember later."

"No," he said, his frown deepening. "I… It's the strangest feeling. I had to tell you. It's important." He turned agitated. "How could I forget?"

A beep announced an incoming call. Zavir looked at his wristwatch.

"Excuse me." He turned his back on them, moving toward the corner as he replied in his language.

"It's a horrible feeling, Liv," Karl said, more animated now.

"It's all right." She took her brother's hand. "Don't think about it now."

"It's important."

"Karl, please. You're repeating yourself."

He grabbed his head between his hands. "What's

wrong with me? Liv, what's going on? Why can't I remember?"

She looked at Zavir in alarm, who'd ended his call.

Karl pushed to his feet. "I have to find Erik. He'll tell me."

"Karl, please." She got up, too, trying to take his arm, but he pulled away. "Where's Erik?"

Zavir said something in Krinar. He moved to Liv's side, putting his arm around her shoulders. She tried to shake him off, to go back to Karl, but he tightened his grip. Xita entered briskly, a pen-like device in her hand.

"What are you doing?" Liv exclaimed.

She strained in Zavir's hold, but he held her firmly while Xita pushed the pen against Karl's arm.

"Hey," he cried, "why did you do that?"

Xita addressed Zavir. "It seems there are some irregularities to iron out."

Karl went limp. Liv reached for him, but Zavir held her back. Before Karl could hit the ground, a long float drifted under him, catching his collapsing body.

"What have you done to him?"

"We'll fix it," Xita said to Zavir.

Liv was beside herself. "Stop ignoring me like I'm not here, damn you."

"Get her out of here," Xita said. "She doesn't want to see this."

"I'm not going anywhere until I have an explanation."

Zavir pushed her toward the door. "Let's go."

She dug her heels in. "No."

Zavir's eyes sparked. "It wasn't a request, Liv."

"Go to hell. You're not the boss of me."

That spark ignited, setting off a look so dark she took a step back.

"Think again," he said, a cold smile playing on his lips.

His arm came behind her knees, and before she could contemplate the move, he scooped her up and threw her over his shoulder.

She banged on his back as he walked to the door. "Put me down!"

Instead of replying, he increased his pace, jostling her none too gently. From her upside-down position, she saw an amused grin spreading over Xita's face. It only infuriated her more.

"Put me down. I can walk."

"You had your chance."

"Where are you going?"

"Where do you think?"

"To my prison," she replied bitterly.

"Clever kitten," he purred.

"What are you going to do?" she asked with a tinge of panic, not wanting to be locked up again.

"I told you there'd be consequences for bad behavior."

Chapter Twelve

Zavir dumped her in the living area of his quarters. The way he watched her promised nothing good, but she was beyond caring. All she could think of was Karl.

He closed the step between them. "Apologize."

"What?" She uttered a hysterical laugh. "You kidnapped me. You said you wouldn't hurt my family." Her voice wavered. "You screwed up. Whatever you're doing to Karl isn't working."

"It's a glitch."

"A glitch?" She stared at him in horror. "He's not a machine that you can reprogram to fix a *glitch*."

"He doesn't deserve your concern."

"He's my brother."

"A brother who hurt you."

"He did what he believed was right."

"Torturing you?"

She flinched. "That was Hans."

"Makes no difference who held the whip or knife. Your brothers allowed it. That makes them no different than

Hans." He spat out the name, his eyes sparking with that undertone of blueish-purple as he said it.

"They didn't know Hans was going to torture me. He was only supposed to scare me. I'm not saying what they did is right. I understand why they did it. I gave them no choice. It doesn't mean I love them less."

"Human love." He scoffed. "How can you love someone so undeserving of it?"

"You don't have siblings, do you?"

"No. Most Krinar don't."

"Then I don't expect you to understand."

She turned away from him, but he grabbed her wrist.

"The only thing I understand is actions and consequences. They let Hans hurt you. They deserve to be punished."

Her anger flared. "Is that what your female friend is doing? Punishing them?"

"Far from. She's trying to help."

"Well, it's not working."

"You made the deal, Liv. You knew what you signed up for."

She pulled on his hold. "I didn't sign up for this."

"You did the minute you kissed me in that bar."

"You made me do it," she cried.

His eyes flattened into slits. "You enjoyed it."

"You tricked me."

"You wanted it."

"Fuck you."

"That's three times you've sworn at me."

"Go to hell. Make that four."

His eyes darkened. The slate-gray color turned to an onyx glow. "As you wish."

When he dragged her toward the bedroom, she dug her heels into the carpet, but it was no use. She was no match for a K. He pulled her through the opening in the wall, not stopping until he reached the bed.

Her heart sped up in alarm. "What are you doing?"

"Honoring my promise."

Sitting down on the bed, he flung her over his lap. She tried to roll off, but he wrapped a hand around her neck, pushing her cheek flat on the mattress.

"Keep still," he ordered, "or I'll add more lashings to your punishment."

"You can't be serious."

She slapped at him, but he easily caught her wrists in one hand, pushing them against her back. Letting go of her neck, he pulled the skirt of her dress up over her waist.

"Ready, kitten?"

"Go fuck yourself."

He sighed. "You've just upped your spanking to ten lashes. Two for each insult. Want to carry on?"

She bit her lip, fuming. There was a lot more she wanted to add, but there was no point in being spiteful to her own detriment.

The first slap on the globe of her ass caught her by surprise. It came too fast, and it hurt like hell. The thin fabric of her panties wasn't much of a barrier. The sting penetrated her skin and traveled all the way to her heart. She swallowed her cry, not wanting to give him the satisfaction of her pain, but the next spank was already heating her skin, making it impossible to hold back her tears. He brought his palm down in a fast succession of swats. She clenched her ass and turned her face into the mattress, grinding her teeth. She'd rather swallow the sheet than utter a sound. It didn't hurt like the whipping she'd taken, far from it, but it wasn't the physical pain that was most damaging. It was the humiliation. She hated herself for the weakness of her tears. She hated her helplessness as she was forced to lie there and take her discipline like a disobedient animal. No, lower than an animal, because she'd never treat an animal with such cruelty.

By the time she'd counted to ten, her ass was on fire and the sheet underneath her wet with her tears. Still, she didn't make a sound.

Zavir's hand smoothed over her bruised skin. "You've been a good, brave little kitten." He turned her over, her burning ass cushioned in his groin. He brushed a tear from her cheek with his thumb. "You took your punishment well."

She turned her face away from his touch. "Let me go."

"I'm not done with you, yet."

Alarm fluttered in her chest. She tried to sit up, but he pinned her wrists down next to her face, moving from under her to roll his body over hers. He licked a tear from her cheek, following it up with soft kisses. The gentle act caught her off balance. Somehow, it intensified the hurt in her heart.

"You're no different than Hans," she whispered, bitterness infusing her tone.

"I'm not him."

"Just because you didn't use a whip doesn't mean you hurt me less."

He pulled away to look at her, his expression surprised. "I didn't inflict damage. You won't have a single bruise."

"I'm not an animal. I have feelings."

For a moment, his eerie eyes searched her face, and then his lips came down on hers, soft and tender, like his earlier caresses. She could handle his cruelty, but not his tenderness. Not after what he'd done. She made a protesting sound, but he only deepened the kiss, parting her lips with his tongue. Heat gathered in her belly. She didn't want to respond to him in this way, but she couldn't help it, not when he kissed her with so much skill, as if he loved savoring her. Despite herself, her body started relaxing, soaking up his heat. As if sensing her dwindling resistance, he let go of her wrists to cup her face.

"My beautiful kitten," he whispered. "You're mine to punish, because you belong to me."

The words jarred her. They made her mind rebel, but her body was boneless, under his spell. It reacted to him as he smoothed a palm up her arm, over her shoulder, and down to her breast. Her hips met his as he ground down softly, letting her feel his erection. She moaned as his hand slipped up her thigh, finding her core. He outlined her folds through her underwear, the touch too soft for what she needed, for what he made her crave.

"Tell me you don't want this," he challenged, tracing her clit.

She blinked at him, bringing his face back into focus through the haze of her arousal.

He rotated his hips. "Tell me you don't feel it."

Satisfaction bled into his eyes when she cried out.

"Thought so."

He kissed her again and, while doing so, ripped off her underwear. Their clothes followed suit. The roughness of the act contrasted with the tender way he claimed her lips, sending confusing signals to her body and brain. The gentleness prevented her from pushing him away, while the urgency with which he parted her thighs made her burn hotter.

"I'm going to fuck you, Liv," he said into their kiss. "Tell me you understand."

She moaned, managing a nod, but he pulled away.

"Say it, kitten. There'll be no misunderstanding, this time. I won't let you accuse me of tricking you, again."

She should say no, but she wanted this. Was she brave enough to admit it?

The answer left her lips in a breathless gasp. "Yes."

The single word was all the permission he needed. His caresses turned more urgent. He plundered her mouth while dragging his palms over her breasts, but kept the same soft pace from before. He took his time with her. She was slick when he positioned his cock at her entrance. Watching her with intense concentration, he penetrated her slowly, giving her enough time to adjust, enough so the stretch didn't hurt.

"Like this?" His breath fanned over her face. "Does it feel good?"

She arched her back and wrapped her legs around him, gripping his hair and tightening her inner muscles.

A low groan escaped him. He thrust deeper. She couldn't take more. The need to come was overwhelming, but he was not to be rushed. As her orgasm neared, she clung to him, needing his broad frame and strong body to protect her from something she didn't understand but instinctively knew could shatter her. Her womb clenched as he moved in sync with her. Pleasure started building slowly. Her breath caught as he hit a sensitive spot.

"Yes," he whispered, his voice sweet and gentle. "Give me what I want."

He kissed her like he was taking her, slowly and carefully. His hands framed her face, tenderly. Her orgasm built just like that—unhurried and intense. When the pleasure exploded, she wrapped her legs tighter around him, needing him deeper and longer and in places she shouldn't.

"Zavir."

He stilled, his face pulling into a grimace of ecstasy. He filled her without breaking their stare, allowing her to witness him in a raw moment of unmasked sensation. The moment of physical bonding was both primal and delicate. It was both satisfying and unfulfilling, making her long for what went beyond the physical, but he was already pulling out, leaving her cold.

He sat up between her legs. "You did beautifully."

The statement was like a clinical evaluation of an act that was supposed to hold more meaning than satiating mutual lust.

The satisfied expression on his face turned into a frown. "Does it hurt?"

"Not physically."

He studied the juncture of her legs. Feeling the evidence of his climax running between her thighs, her cheeks heated.

When he looked back at her, the pleased look returned to his eyes, but there was also something else–a quiet discord.

Unable to prevent herself, she reached out to trace his birthmark, or his defect, as he'd put it. "How long are you planning on keeping me here?"

"I haven't decided. It depends."

"On what?"

"Many things."

"Such as?"

"Your safety. How quickly you adapt. My future missions."

"Wait." He'd also mentioned her safety before going to see her brother. "Is there something else I should know that concerns my safety?"

He shifted farther away but kept his hand on her leg. "There are rumors."

"What rumors?" She pushed up on her elbows. "Don't make me drag everything out of you. Just say it."

His gaze softened. No, it wasn't softness she saw in his eyes. It was an apology. "There are still a few Resistance supporters on the loose, people whose names were not in the files you gave us. They put a price on your head. They're angry about what you did. News got out."

"The guy from the bar?" she said as she put two and two together. "The one Hans paid for information?"

He stroked her calf. "That's the word around town, yes."

There was more. "Your people—they want me dead, too?"

"You're an informant. Some think you could be double-crossing us."

That didn't sound good for her future. It wasn't something she'd considered, not that it would've changed her decision. "Does that mean I'll have to look over my shoulder for the rest of my life?"

He squeezed her ankle. "You have nothing to fear. I'll protect you."

Which brought her back to the question he hadn't answered. "How long am I supposed to stay here? Eventually, you'll let me go, right?" *Even charl have freedom, don't they?*

His eyes darkened, the color looking like coals glowing with blue flames. "I'm not letting you go."

"What?" she cried softly. "As in a week, a month? Give me a timeline. A year?"

His cold gaze bored into hers. "As in forever."

Chapter Thirteen

His little human wasn't happy. No, far from it. Why did it make him so angry? What did he expect? Gratitude? Acceptance? He'd known back in the bar her life would be in danger from all sides, human and Krinar alike. He couldn't allow that. He'd known then, even before he'd kissed her, that to keep her safe he had to make her his. He'd known she was a tough one from the minute he'd seen her press a knife to that sleazy traitor's testicles. He'd known taming her wouldn't be easy, but when he'd kissed her, he'd forgotten about all of that. The only knowledge that had stuck in his mind was that he was going to take her. Claim her. That, he'd done. The evidence was still dribbling from her sex. This time, she'd enjoyed it, too.

He'd been more careful, reminding himself how fragile she was. In his lust-filled haze, it wasn't easy. When he was inside her body, it was difficult to focus on anything other than her tight grip on his cock. It was difficult to behave responsibly, let alone think. The pretty vixen with her soft curves and responsive body was monopolizing his mind.

She clouded his judgment. He shouldn't be angry at her for her defiance over staying with him, but he couldn't help it. The rejection stung. He needed distance to cool down.

He pushed from the bed, turning his back on her.

Her voice shook a little. "Zavir?"

"What?" he snapped. "Is there something you need?"

She wasn't to be deterred by his attitude. Oh, no. The pretty human climbed from the bed and came to stand in front of him. Naked. Zut, he couldn't reason when she confronted him with that voluptuous body, still wet from their sex. He wanted to do it again and worse. He wanted to do much worse to her. He wanted to fuck her senseless. He wanted to bite her and make them both fly so high she'd never question her place by his side again.

"Forever?" she whispered.

He forced his gaze to her eyes, lest he bend her over the bed and take her harder than what she could handle. "For as long as I'll live."

"That's a very long time. I'll be old before. What will you do with me when I'm a shriveled, eighty-year-old woman?"

"You won't be."

"Humans grow old, Zavir."

"I gave you nanocytes when I healed you. Any deteriorating or damaged cells in your body will regenerate themselves."

Her pretty face paled. "I–I'll live as long as you?"

"Yes. We both have eternal lifespans. We can still die if injured fatally, but we won't perish from sickness or age."

She covered her mouth with a hand. "You didn't ask me. Maybe I don't want to live that long."

"It's done. Your place is at my side."

She dropped her hand. "Forever."

"That's what I said."

"I'll outlive everyone I love." Her eyes filled with sadness. "I'll see them grow old and die."

"I know it'll be hard, but it's inevitable. I'll be here for you. How does the human saying go? We'll cross that bridge when we get there."

"You had no right to make such a decision on my behalf."

"Liv, stop it. You're my charl. I had every right. We're not talking about this, any longer. If there's nothing else, I have things to do."

"Actually, there is."

"Go on, then."

"Karl said something about an engagement."

He felt another rejection coming. "What about it?"

She flinched at his tone. "When is it supposed to take place?"

"In a month's time."

When she'd had time to get more comfortable with the idea. He liked the human custom. Since they couldn't formalize their union in Krinar fashion, which was only reserved for Krinar mates, a human engagement would have to do. A ring on her finger would show all males she belonged to him. Who knew? Maybe in forty-seven years' time there would be a formal union for cheren and charl. "I'm throwing a big party as per the human custom. I want every Krinar and influential human to attend, including your ambassador."

"Why?"

"I'll make a public announcement about taking you as charl at the party. I want everyone on Earth to know. I want it all over the news."

It would serve as a warning to anyone who had as much as an inkling to harm Liv. They'd know if they touched his charl, he'd kill them.

"When were you going to tell me?"

What was the point if she was only going to say no? He hardened his heart. Going soft because of a human woman wasn't going to help either of them survive. "Does it matter?"

She reeled as if he'd slapped her. "We're talking about my life."

"Which I now own."

"Oh, that's right." Her blue eyes turned bright, a spark flashing in their depths. "Because I'm a pet to amuse you?"

"If you already know the answer, why do you ask?"

She shook her head, a tear slipping over her cheek. "You're so cruel."

She accused him of cruelness when her own kind had damaged her in the most horrifying way, when he saved her?

He clenched his fists to keep from touching her. "Get used to it."

Her cheeks turned pink, and her nostrils flared. "It's not what I want."

He laughed softly. "Liar."

She all but blew smoke from her nose like a dragon. "I'm not the liar here."

"Is that right?"

His patience snapped. Wrapping his hand around her neck, he backed her up to the wall. A puff of air left her lips when her body connected with the surface. He dragged his nose along the column of her neck, inhaling the fragrance of her skin. He registered the shiver that ran over her body with satisfaction, because it proved his point.

"You don't want this?" he asked, licking a path along her skin.

She gasped.

His fingers found a hardened nipple and pinched softly. "How about this?"

"Zavir." His name was a protest, but she leaned into the touch.

He moved his hand between their bodies to cup her sex, swollen and wet from their fucking. "Or this?"

She pushed her hips back, trying to escape the touch, but when he touched her clit, she moaned.

He slipped two fingers inside her. "This?"

She arched her back, thrusting her hips. He stroked her inside, letting her feel the pleasure, letting her become as wild as she was making him. When he pulled out, she protested again, but for a different reason. As little as she wanted to admit it, they wanted the same thing. He kicked her legs apart and grabbed his erection in his hand.

"How about this?" he asked, rubbing the head over her slick folds.

Her nails dug into his shoulders. "Zavir."

"What, kitten?" he taunted. "You don't like it?"

"That's not what I—"

The rest of her words were cut off when he speared into her, taking everything in one go. "Or did you mean this?"

"Zavir." There was desperation in her tone. "Stop it."

He didn't know if she meant the sex or the words that proved her wrong, but there was no stopping. Not any longer, not now that her heat drenched him and her muscles flexed in a way that promised both their release.

He thrust into her, not gentle and kind, but with punishing strokes, strokes evoked from the madness she woke inside him.

"This?" he asked, keeping up the grueling pace. "Stop this?"

Her legs buckled. "Oh, God. No."

He gripped her hips to keep her up. "What was that, kitten?"

"Zavir," she said on a defeated sob.

"Say it," he insisted.

"No." Her head fell back. "No, damn you. Don't stop."

Victory was bittersweet. He'd proven what he wanted, but why did it feel like he'd lost a battle? There was no time to analyze the thought. She lifted one leg around him, taking him deeper. It drove him insane. He wanted to show her how good it could be, if she'd only stop resisting him so hard. The pleasure was unlike any he'd experienced, jostling his mind with an unfounded fear. This little human could be his undoing. He wanted far more than she was willing to give. It didn't matter. In time, he'd make her realize there was no other choice. He was doing what he was doing in her best interest, or so he told himself.

She cried out under him, desperate sounds that gave voice to the feverish build of his own need. All logic and thoughts flew to the moon. Instinct took over, a primal force driving him to claim the woman who didn't want to be claimed. At least, not by him. His hips pivoted with brutal force, taking what was his. Taking what wasn't his. He held her in place as he showed her everything they both wanted, because their bodies didn't lie. Answering a call from deep inside not to let go, he tightened his hold, and dragged his tongue over her neck to taste her skin. When she whimpered, he sealed his lips over hers to catch the sound, wanting everything and still some.

The kiss was too rough. A coppery taste told him he'd cut her lip with his teeth. From a distant corner of his mind, a voice told him to slow down, but it was already too much. Her slickness, her heat, her tightening channel, the taste of her blood… She stole his reason. He kissed a path to the curve of her shoulder, sucking and nipping. Her moans told him how much she liked it, too. Without thinking, he laved the spot with his tongue, preparing her, and sliced his teeth across her skin.

She jerked in his hold, and they both exploded. He came harder than ever, his pleasure an uncontainable and inexhaustible eruption that stretched on and on, into exhaustion, until even his powerful legs couldn't hold them up. Liv had long since gone limp in his arms, her body convulsing as multiple climaxes shattered them both. He barely had the strength to lower them to the floor. It went on for hours. He was no longer the master of his body. Fucking was a need like breathing, and he could only breathe with her. The need was excruciating. It refused to let him go. Over and over, he took her, fucked her, and filled her, until her voice was hoarse and her body drenched in sweat. It was never enough. After every climax, he needed more.

It was only when the darkness faded, and the rosy glow of sunrise touched the transparent ceiling that his need diminished, and he started feeling more like himself. Pushing up onto his elbows, he stared at the face of the woman he'd claimed. Her pale features were still. Her limbs were motionless. She looked exhausted. Her porcelain white skin sported bruises, especially on her hips and between her thighs. This was the woman he'd taken responsibility for, who he'd soon promise to take care of in front of the world as his witness. What had gotten into him?

He'd done what he promised himself he wouldn't. He'd gotten carried away. He'd not been careful. All the gentleness he wanted to shower on her, everything he'd managed at the beginning of the night was blown to the three moons. By zut, she was so tired she looked unconscious. On the zutten floor. He took her like that *on the floor*.

Cursing himself, he picked her up in his arms. She didn't even stir when he carried her to the shower and cleaned her. After laying her carefully on the bed, he used the nano-healer to take away the bruises and bite marks on her shoulder. He took special care with her feminine parts. He wanted her to feel good, not shudder in discomfort after every time he touched her.

Remembering that humans needed much more rest, he drew a blanket over her and left her to sleep. He had work to do, but he could do it from the room next-door to not disturb her. He wanted to be here when she woke. Already, he felt reluctance at being separated from his Earthling. Was this the bond some other Krinar who'd taken mates were talking about?

He settled in the living area to call up the information from the worldwide arrests that had been made as a consequence of the intelligence Liv had provided. It went deeper than he could've imagined. As he'd told her, not all the Resistance members had been uncovered. There were still a few rotten apples. Before he could pull up the information Korum had sent, a hologram came to life with an incoming message. Xita's face appeared in the space.

"I'm busy, Xita."

"You'd want to hear this."

He tensed, stealing a glance at the bedroom where his charl was sleeping. "How's Karl?"

"He escaped."

Chapter Fourteen

L ike the first morning, Liv woke feeling completely rested. She stretched, reveling in the way the mattress molded to support her body. Her cheeks heated as she recalled how she'd spent the night. Zavir had bitten her. Again. This time it had been incredible, at least the parts she could remember. Everything was a blur. She remembered nothing but pleasure, pleasure so intense she was terrified it would destroy her, but then she recalled their words, and her smile faded. Then she looked at the empty space next to her, and her heart chilled.

Getting out of bed, she checked her body. Her skin was smooth and flawless. Some of her freckles had even disappeared. Like the day before, her appetite was healthy, reminding her she was starving. She had no watch or phone to tell the time, but through the ceiling, the sun was sitting high.

"Time, please," she said.

A digital number appeared on the wall, announcing an hour well after lunch. Had she really been sleeping all day?

After dressing, she asked the house for a late lunch. It

delivered a delicious, hearty Krinar stew, which it announced as Kalfani. While the house cleaned itself, she paced. Zavir was probably working. She longed for news from Karl and Erik. Zavir had said she could call him, but she didn't feel like asking him for anything, especially not news about her brothers. An idea occurred to her.

"I want to speak to Karl in the medical center," she told the house. "Karl Madsen."

Nothing.

"Xita?"

Still nothing.

She guessed communication with anyone other than Zavir wasn't one of her liberties.

With nothing else to do, she settled on a long float and asked for the tablet, which the house produced promptly. She requested the latest news sites, reading with increasing concern about the fall of the Resistance cell, the arrests of the parties involved, and the continued uncovering of more members, but there was nothing about her family except for one line that said the Resistance members had been rehabilitated.

The hours dragged on with her pacing, lying on the bed staring at the transparent ceiling, or trying to read, but she couldn't focus on anything. The silence and worry were killing her.

"Music," she finally said in an effort not to go out of her mind.

One of her favorite songs came on, playing through the living quarters.

"How did you know I like that song?" she asked the house.

Silence.

She sighed. "It was worth a try."

She walked around the rooms again–bedroom,

dressing room, bathroom, living area, and kitchen. Bedroom, dressing room, bathroom, living area, kitchen. Round and round like a caged animal.

"Can we have a conversation?" she asked in desperation into the space.

"What would you like to converse about?" a pleasant, female voice responded.

"I don't know." She flopped down on a plank. "Anything."

"Please select a subject."

"Have you known Zavir for long?"

Silence.

"I get it. You're not allowed to give me information about him. How about the recent Resistance arrests?"

Nothing.

"Okay. Tell me about the food on Krina. The Kalfani was delicious."

"I am sorry. Krina related information is confidential."

"Ah, I see. I'm a spy, right? You can't trust me."

More silence.

"I suppose you're not going to tell me anything about our engagement party plans, either?"

No reply.

Talking to the house wasn't working. She went back to walking in circles, feeling her mind turn in much the same way, until the sky once more became dark and the exterior wall finally disintegrated to let Zavir in.

He stopped when he saw her in the lounge. His unsettling gaze roamed over her, as if he was doing inventory of her body. Strain tinged his deep voice. "How are you doing?"

"I'm fine."

"I'm glad to see you've eaten well."

"How did you–?" She stopped abruptly as she realized

the answer. Of course. The house. "How does it work? Do you get a detailed report on my calorie intake? How many times I use the bathroom?"

He closed the distance between them and stopped in front of her. "It's in your best interest that I know what you consume and how long you rest."

"What do you care?"

He brushed his knuckles over her cheek. "You're my responsibility. Your health is my concern."

"Oh, I get it. I need to be in good shape for a repeat of last night."

He dropped his hand. "We won't be doing that for a while."

"Why? Isn't that why you're keeping me?"

His jaw clenched. "If we do it too often, we'll get addicted."

She gave a cynical laugh. "Ah and I won't serve your purpose if I'm a sex addict."

"Not the sex, my bite."

"Damn." She adopted a mocking tone. "For a moment I thought we didn't have to have sex tonight."

He moved so fast, she was pushed up against the float before she could blink.

"Why are you making this so hard on yourself?" he asked through tight lips, his arms caging her in. "We've been through this, but if it's a game you like playing, I can indulge you. We can start at square one, with me proving to you what you like. Is that what you want?"

His voice had lowered an octave, but the soft-spoken tone didn't hide the anger that flashed in his eyes. No, he'd made his point. She didn't want a repeat only to suffer the humiliation of how defenseless she was to his touch, how easily she came apart under his hands.

"No," she whispered, "I don't want that."

He didn't ease up. "Good." Tension vibrated from his body. "We're going to settle this for once and all. I want to hear you say it."

She stared up at his eyes, seeing nothing but the turbulent storm brewing within. "Say what?"

"Admit you want me."

It was the truth. They both knew it, but a rebellious part of her made her ask, "Why?"

"I don't want to take one step forward with you only to take two back every time." When she didn't answer, he continued, "Make no mistake, I'll go back to step one as many times as it takes."

Her shoulders slumped. "Fine. The attraction is mutual."

"Say it out straight, Liv, not in a roundabout way."

"I want you. Happy?"

"That's better. Was that so hard?"

He had no idea.

"Now that's out of the way," he said, "how about dinner?"

"I'm not hungry. I'm sure you know I ate not so long ago."

Ignoring the bite in her words, he stepped back, setting her free. It was almost like a give and take, like she'd given him something, and he'd given her something in return. She just couldn't define what he'd given her.

"What would you like to do?" he asked.

Her laugh was bitter. "You're giving me a choice?"

His expression darkened, but his tone remained even. "What do you do to relax? Maybe you'd like to watch a movie or play chess."

She loved chess. The simple fact that he knew infuriated her for reasons she couldn't fathom. Anyway, what was the point? She'd never have a fair game against a K.

Their intelligence was superior, wasn't it? Like with every-thing else, she'd always lose, unless he faked it. The thought sent a wave of rage through her. Much more devastating was the sadness it evoked.

The latter made her say, "No sex? May as well get it over with. That's what I'm for, isn't it?"

Sparks detonated in his eyes. They narrowed to slits as his cheekbones darkened. "As you wish." His tone was cold and impersonal. "Lie down on the bed and spread your legs."

It was a self-induced punishment, a self-destructive move, but her legs shook nevertheless as she walked to the bedroom. She wasn't going to make it easy for him. She didn't undress before lying down in the center of the bed.

If she hoped to make it difficult by forcing him to remove her clothes, she was sadly disappointed. He flipped her skirt over her hips as he climbed between her legs, sparing her not a single look as he pushed her underwear aside and expertly fingered her clit. His movements were sparse and clinical. He got her wet, but there was nothing erotic or romantic about it. When her channel was slick, he pushed into her, taking her with the same mechanical, emotionless efficiency. For all his lack of feeling, she made up for it in abundance, her sadness at the pinnacle as she came despite his coldness. Her shame at how hard she climaxed while he used her as nothing but a vessel in which to empty his release didn't fall far behind. When he got up and went to the bathroom to clean himself, she remained in the puddle of shame and self-loathing in his bed, filled with his seed, and left so empty.

A short while later, he walked from the bathroom, freshly showered and dressed. He paused at the side of the bed to look down at her. Two, three heartbeats passed, and then he left the room. Silence stretched through the space.

What was she supposed to do? She could stay there and wallow in her shame or follow him and make the best of the situation until she figured out a solution. A bargain. An escape. Letting the resolution strengthen her, she got up, took a few minutes to clean up in the bathroom, and went through to the living area, but it was empty.

He was gone.

———

THE WAY ZAVIR stalked into the meeting room demonstrated his lack of constraint, but he couldn't make himself care. All he could think about was the obstinate woman in his quarters who accepted him with her body and rejected him with everything else. The two people around the float– Xita and Korum–studied him with interest. Their curiosity only irked him more.

"Love trouble?" Xita asked on a chuckle.

"If you know what's good for you, you'll keep quiet now," he growled.

She snickered. "The man who single-handedly took down armies can't tame his charl."

"Xita," Korum said, giving her a warning look.

Best get to the point, so that he could get back to his charl. He didn't like the way he'd left her, but she needed to understand he wouldn't stand for her little rebellions. "What do we know about Karl?"

"Erik and Hans are gone too," Xita said. "I found their holding room empty just after you'd left us this evening, a couple of Earth hours ago."

"What?" he asked with disbelief.

"Someone let them out," Korum said, his face tight. "There's no other way they could've escaped from the medical center."

"Someone who knew how to remove their shinings and wipe out the security feed," Xita added.

Zavir rubbed his temples. "Any suspects?"

Xita shook her head. "None. We checked all the staff that had access to the medical center. There's more. Their rehabilitation hasn't been completed." Xita looked between him and Korum. "It looks as if someone reversed the procedure. Their memories have been restored."

"Therefore, technically, all three are guilty," Korum concluded. "They didn't just walk out of here with someone believing they're on holiday. They know they escaped."

"Still no trace of them?" Zavir asked.

"Nothing," Xita replied.

Zavir had considered all angles, and it always came back to this. It was the only plausible theory. "Someone on the inside is working for the Resistance."

Korum got to his feet and walked to the wall, which turned transparent to give him a one-way view of the meeting center garden. "I want the traitor found." He rounded, his eyes on Zavir, the command in them unques-tionable. "Without delay."

"How do you suppose I do that? Have everyone take a lie detector test? With the amount of Ks in here, it will take ages."

"It's not what I had in mind."

Zavir raised a brow, waiting in silence.

Korum's smile was calculated. "We're going to use your informant as bait."

Chapter Fifteen

"No." Zavir planted his fist on the float. "It'll put her life in danger."

Korum's golden eyes darkened. "It's an order."

"It's dangerous," Zavir insisted.

"She's an *informant*," the leader said.

"Who helped us."

Undeterred, Korum turned for the exit. "I'll send instructions."

"Mia was an informant, and worse, for her own kind, against us, yet you forgave her."

Korum spun around. He looked like a tiger ready to attack. "Do you have a problem with my charl?"

"No," Zavir replied quietly. "I'm only asking for your understanding."

At that, Korum stilled. He seemed to consider the words for a while, his body slowly relaxing.

"Fine," he said at large. "Your engagement party is in a month's time. You have until then to find the traitor."

Zavir nodded his gratitude.

When the leader was gone, Xita regarded Zavir curiously.

"What are you going to tell your charl?" she asked.

His tone was clipped. "Nothing."

"What if she asks to see her brothers?"

"I'll tell her to wait. I'll find them, one way or another. For your sake, I hope you'll have better results with the rehabilitation then."

Her lips curved into a smile. "I will. The data mining, though, was impeccable."

"Did you extract all the information?"

"Everything on the Resistance."

"And?"

"As I said, confidential."

"Nothing I should know?"

"If the Council wants you to know, you will."

He was tempted to push her, because where Liv was concerned he could never learn enough, but she was right. His job was to execute cleanup missions, not analyze intel. Still, he didn't like being in the dark, and he had a feeling he was not only navigating his way through the dark, but also doing it blindfolded. Especially where his human was concerned. He had no idea how to make her accept the inevitable. He was running out of ideas, and now also out of time, thanks to Korum's deadline. The knowledge weighed on his shoulders as he made for the exit, suddenly eager to get back to Liv.

"Zavir."

He paused, waiting for Xita to continue.

"I'm on your side."

Giving her a look from over his shoulder, he said, "I know."

———

TIME AND MORE TIME. That was all Liv had. After being busy every minute of every day, doing nothing was getting to her. After the expanse of the South African desert and the Costa Rican jungle, being locked up in an off-white room with off-white furniture and off-white fixings didn't help. She paced, and read, and paced. She watched news broadcasts and paced some more. She had a lot of time to think.

There was no point in resisting Zavir. He'd proven his point. Too well. Turning into a puddle of lust under his hands made her cheeks burn in shame. Insulting him resulted in a humiliating spanking. Fighting him didn't accomplish anything, either. His punishment for that was far more effective than a spanking or gleeful seduction. When he'd reduced her being to nothing but an object it hurt. He'd made his point. The choice was in her hands. She could either enjoy sex with him, allowing him to make it incredible or only hurt herself by letting him keep it cold. No matter what she chose, sex was going to happen. That, he'd proven, too. Why fight a losing battle?

Escaping from Lenkarda was impossible. She knew better than anyone the place was a fortress. Hadn't the Resistance searched for ways in for months? Even if she did manage to get away, she wouldn't get far. Not with a tracker. For now, she had no choice but to make the best of being Zavir's prisoner, but did she want to get engaged to him? Did she want to be his charl? When he announced it at their engagement party, she'd be irrevocably bound to him for life. He'd never be able to turn his back on her, whereas without too many people knowing yet, he could still denounce her as his charl. Maybe he'd tire of her. Could she convince him not to go ahead with the announcement? In the light of the situation, asking for more time wasn't unreasonable.

She was still contemplating her options, or lack of them, when Zavir returned. If he harbored any grudges about the way she'd reacted or how he'd left, he didn't show it. His gaze homed in on her. For a long moment, he did nothing but stare at her. She got to her feet and went to him, stopping close enough that she had to crane her neck to look at his face. His eyes flared in surprise. He'd clearly not expected her to come to him. Maybe they could have that dinner he'd mentioned, and she'd tried to behave in a civil way and ask him for time.

"When will you have your next meal?" she asked.

He traced her cheek with his knuckles, his gaze softening. "Not for a while."

"Oh."

"We don't have to refuel as often as you."

She bit her lip. "I know." Okay, dinner could wait.

"Are you hungry?"

"Not yet."

From the way his eyes darkened as they roamed over her, she knew what he wanted. Most of all, she knew because she wanted it, too. Their chemistry was undeniable. That was true, but it took more than chemistry to forge a life-long bond.

Turning on her heel, she walked to the bedroom. She didn't have to look over her shoulder to know he'd followed. She could feel him standing on the threshold, watching her as she pushed the dress from her shoulders and let it fall at her feet. She wasn't wearing a bra. Her panties followed next. He let out a hiss when she bent over to free her feet from the underwear. Before she could climb onto the bed, he was behind her, folding his large body over hers. Her breathing quickened as his hands slid down her back to cup her ass. He pulled her open, exposing her for his eyes. It made her feel more naked than ever, having her need splayed and laid at his feet, having him witness her arousal.

He dragged a finger through her slit, gathering her wetness. More proof. More evidence. She closed her eyes as he palmed a breast while pushing a digit inside her channel. Torturously slow, he moved his finger, finding the sensitive spot that made her back arch. As she pushed into him, he grunted his approval. He abandoned her breast to brush her hair over her shoulder and dragged a thumb over the spot where he'd bitten her. A shiver ran over her back. Goosebumps broke out over her arm. He kissed the spot tenderly. She expected him to bite again, but he only kept his lips there for a few seconds, all the while teasing her with his finger.

"Zavir."

He kissed the shell of her ear. "What do you need, kitten?"

"More."

His answer was to pull out of her. She moaned in disappointment, looking over her shoulder at him. There was a blur of movement, and then he was naked, aligning his erection with her slit. He pressed in slowly, caressing her breast and clit, taking his time. He was excruciatingly gentle, studying the place where their bodies were joined with unwavering concentration. Watching him watching them fuck was so hot. His cheekbones darkened, and the color of his eyes turned to a molten iron. Her slickness eased his movements, allowing him to go faster and deeper.

"Make me come," she demanded, breathing heavily.

He didn't hesitate to fulfill her wish. Pinching her clit between a forefinger and thumb, he rolled the nub gently. The spasm of pleasure that contracted the muscles in her lower region was instantaneous. She came on the spot, tightening around him and provoking his curse. Her legs started shaking. Snaking an arm around her waist, he lifted her higher onto the mattress without breaking their connection. He increased the pace. Her passage slickened more, and her folds swelled. The pleasure was unbearable.

"I can't," she whimpered.

He freed his cock. His command was staccato, his voice strained. "On your back."

When he released her, she rolled over to face him.

"Spread your legs, kitten. I want to look."

She opened her legs. He looked until he had his fill, slowly shifting his eyes up until their gazes locked. He didn't break the stare as he pushed back into her and started a new pace, more urgent than before. She wrapped her legs around him. He intertwined their fingers and lifted her hands above her head. They were wound around and into each other.

"I can fuck you like this all day long," he murmured, hitting her sweet spot.

She cried out, rolling her hips to meet his rhythm. Already, her channel tightened.

"Yes," he hissed. "That's a good girl. Come with me."

When he roared out his climax, she came around his thickening cock. He swelled and swelled inside her, filling her with warmth and showering her with soft words and tender kisses.

She sighed in bliss. This was so much better than having her skirt hitched up for a cold fuck. It was only lust, but this was mutual. This was them.

———

HIS KITTEN WAS pliant in his arms when he carried her to the shower to clean them both. She was agreeable, like she'd been in bed. The sudden change was welcome.

Alarming, even. It wasn't like Liv to be so docile. He couldn't help being a little worried. When he carried her back to the bedroom and told her to get on her knees, she did so without arguing. She allowed him to fuck her hot mouth, and she swallowed his seed. When he ordered her to bend over, she offered herself to him, moaning as he brought her to an orgasm with his tongue. Even when he commanded her to sit naked on his lap while he read over some reports, she said nothing as his erection grew and jutted, seeking entrance between her thighs. He took her there, on the spot, against his better judgment, knowing he'd have to use the nano-healer again. He laid her down to sleep and pulled her body tight against his. Like the bastard he was, he slipped the ring he'd gotten the day before onto her finger while she was passed out from exhaustion. He wasn't sure he could handle another rejection. He had the thick skin many humans and Krinar accused him of having, but he had no protection where his charl was concerned. As far as she went, his heart was naked, an open target, too prone to bleeding. Although he didn't need the rest, he stayed with her, enjoying the feel of her warm, soft skin and the sound of her breathing. Only when the first rays of the sun entered through the ceiling and she opened her eyes, did he stir.

She blinked, as if surprised to find him there.

"Hey," she said in a cute, shy way.

He brushed a strand of hair from her face. "Morning."

"You stayed."

"I did."

"Why?"

"Do I need a reason to stay with you?"

"It's just…"

"Just what?"

"I know you don't need sleep. Not yet."

"I wasn't sleeping."

She flushed a little. "Oh."

He smiled at her. He liked them like this. Not at war. Then she rubbed her eyes. He knew the exact moment she felt the ring. She froze. Her face lost its blush, turning pale. Her body went rigid. Lifting her hand in the air, she stared at the platinum band with the tanzanite stone. He'd chosen that stone because it looked like the color of her eyes. It had seemed infinitely beautiful to him, but she was regarding it as if it radiated toxic waste.

Her voice was tremulous, and not in a good way. "Zavir."

He couldn't help sounding defensive. "What?"

"Of all the low-life things to do."

Declaring her bond with him in human terms was low-life? He suppressed his anger, trying to look at the situation from her point of view. "I'm sorry it was like this."

"In my sleep?" she asked, her tone bitter.

"I know you deserve better. I'll make up for it with the party. I promise."

Sitting up, she hugged her knees. Her bare back was exposed to him. He trailed a path over the pale skin, his heart clenching when he remembered the blood and deep lines where Hans had tortured her. His nostrils flared at the memory. The mental images were imprinted in his mind, waking a deep rage inside of him.

"Zavir?" She faced him sideways, looking at him from under her lashes.

"Kitten?"

"May I ask you something?"

He traced the delicate line of her spine. "Yes."

Her skin contracted with goose bumps. "The engagement party…"

He tensed, dropping his hand. Their newfound peace wasn't going to last long, after all. "What about it?"

"Does it have to be next month?" She continued quickly. "I mean, can't we wait a bit?"

Pushing away from her, he swung his legs off the bed.

Her voice had a note of desperation. "Zavir."

He kept his back to her, couldn't look at her for the fear of seeing the truth in her eyes. "Is that what last night was about?"

Hurt mixed with the desperation in her tone. "What do you mean?"

"Is that why you came to me out of your own?"

"No," she exclaimed. "I'm not trying to manipulate you with sex."

"What then? Why the sudden rebellion again?"

"It's too much. Too soon." She swallowed audibly. "Maybe you'll grow tired of me."

He uttered a cold laugh. "In your dreams, darling."

"Please, Zavir, is it too much to ask?"

He stood, flexing his hands before curling them into fists. "The party will take place as scheduled."

For a long time, there was only silence. When he finally gathered the courage to face her, she had a smile on her face, but her eyes were misty. Too bright.

"Don't test me, Liv."

"Okay," she said, infusing that same, fake brightness into her tone.

He couldn't stand it, didn't want that layer of pretense between them as little as he wanted a layer of clothes. "Don't lie to me, either."

"I'm only doing what you told me."

"What may that be?"

"Not to make this any harder. Will protesting and screaming help?"

No, it wouldn't, but it bothered him that she felt like protesting. His mood turned sullen. He only had himself to blame. Yes, she was doing exactly what he'd told her. She needed time to adjust to her new circumstances, but it was the one thing not in his power to give. What prevented the Council from taking her away from him? He had to make the fact that he'd claimed her public, and a formal ceremony like an engagement would serve that purpose. Korum could use her as bait, but the Council members would be a lot less comfortable with sacrificing her life if the world knew she belonged to Zavir. No, a month was all she had. All *he* had.

"No," he said, the word hard in its finality. "It won't make a single difference."

She swallowed again and lowered her lashes, hiding her tears.

"Come." He held out his hand in a peace offering. Apology. He couldn't decide. Whatever. As long as he could remove this barrier that now hung heavy between them. "You need breakfast."

She took his hand but shook her head. "Thank you, but I'm not hungry."

His fingers tightened on hers. "You have to eat."

"Maybe later."

The words were weak, a poor assurance, but he didn't have the heart to push her after their exchange as little as he could help being angry at her for trying to escape that knot that would tie her to him indefinitely. He was a mass of conflicting emotions, and he hated it. He released her hand.

"Zavir, I…"

His impatience sounded like rudeness. "Was there something else?"

She winced. "I…yes."

"I don't have all day." What had gotten into him? *Calm the zut down.* She didn't deserve this. It wasn't her fault.

Her eyes grew large, but she ploughed on. "I was wondering... May I please see Karl again? And Erik?"

"No."

More hurt washed into her beautiful eyes.

"When, then?"

"When the time is right."

"Why? Is something wrong?"

"Nothing you need to concern yourself about."

"This is it?" she asked softly, a quiver to her voice. "This is how it's going to be?"

"I've already told you, how it's going to be depends entirely on you."

The wounded look on her face was as much as he could take. Not trusting his temper, he got dressed and left to start the task of finding their Keith.

———

As THE DAYS PASSED, Liv's appetite dwindled. She was list-less and tired. Her moods hovered between sadness and desperation, because Zavir wouldn't tell her anything about her brothers. Except for that one visit with Karl, she hadn't seen them since Zavir had kidnapped her. She hadn't seen anyone except Zavir. He kept her locked in his quarters, refusing to tell her how long they were staying. For all she knew, she was trapped here indefinitely. She couldn't bring herself to read, watch movies, or try to have a conversation with the house. Since she'd stopped asking the house for meals, it delivered them automatically, always at set mealtimes. She ate for the sole purpose of nourishing her body, but the dresses that had come with the house were already fitting looser.

Zavir worked in the day and came to her at night, adjusting his calendar to her human hours and the physical demands of her body. He took her every night, sometimes several times. She couldn't blame his healthy libido for being tired. What else did she have to do but rest? Only, sleep didn't come easily. Like her appetite, it was something that had started eluding her.

Making a point of keeping track of time, she asked the house for the date every morning. Today was Friday. She lay in bed, rubbing her eyes while gathering the energy to get up and dress. Even the mundane tasks seemed too demanding. She dragged herself to the bathroom, showered, and dressed, like every other morning, and then went to the living area where breakfast would be waiting, like every other morning. A huge bouquet of pink roses made her stop in her tracks.

Her favorite.

The perfume of the flowers drifted to her on the air. She approached the float on which the vase stood. They were magnificent. Running a finger over the velvet petals, she inhaled their sweet scent. Her gaze fell on the float set with breakfast. It wasn't the dishes from Krina she'd gotten used to, but a stack of pancakes drenched in syrup and topped with fat, ripe strawberries. Next to it stood a steaming mug of coffee.

Her favorite breakfast.

She padded to the table, taking in the feast.

"What's the occasion?"

She didn't expect the house to answer, any longer, but she'd gotten used to talking to herself, voicing her thoughts out loud.

A plank drifted under her, almost encouraging her to sit down. She did so hesitantly, not fully understanding or trusting what was going on. The sight of the food did make her stomach rumble, reminding her she needed to eat, even if she didn't feel like it. Not even the sight of the scrumptious breakfast was enough to kick-start her appetite. She cut into the fluffy pancake and took a small bite. The food smelled good. It was probably delicious, but she tasted nothing. Her stomach protested as she swallowed. She picked off a few strawberries, chewing unenthusiastically.

In the dressing room, a new dress waited for her. It wasn't the pastel colors of the Krinar, but bright red. It was pretty, but she wasn't used to showing so much skin.

At lunchtime, she was taken aback to find a portion of planted-based chicken substitute and French fries on her plate. She ate a few fries and managed to take a couple of bites of the chicken substitute. It tasted good, but she wasn't hungry. She spent the afternoon watching the digital time on the wall, waiting for Zavir to arrive.

When he finally did, she got up from her seat in the lounge, almost too eagerly. The only distraction she could cope with was sex. Wow. Maybe she was turning into a sex addict.

A smile transformed Zavir's face as she neared. She studied his chiseled features, the square jaw darkened with his trimmed beard, straight nose, and angled lines of his cheekbones. Harsh and dangerous, but not at the moment. Now, he regarded her with a warm light in his eyes that softened his features. He was physical perfection, from his broad frame and the lithe way he moved, down to his odd birthmark. The mark only made him more perfect in his uniqueness. He was unlike any other K she knew. Unlike any other man. No one else provoked the tingling feeling in her belly or the warmth that spread through her womb at the knowledge of what was to come. Pathetic as it was, she looked forward to being used, just as she'd be using him for her own pleasure.

He took her hand, but instead of leading her to the bedroom, he pulled her to his chest. "Missed me?" he asked in a low voice, brushing his lips over hers.

The scruffiness of his stubble reminded her of how good that scratchiness felt between her legs. Her cheeks heated at the thought even as her inner muscles clenched.

"You have a beard."

His eyes crinkled in the corners. "You're only noticing now?"

"What I mean to say is you have one when other Ks don't. How come?"

"For the same reason I have a skin defect. I'm not a designer baby conceived in a lab. My conception happened spontaneously."

"That explains the Ks' perfection. Most of them must be designer babies."

"Yes. The imperfect exceptions like me are few and far apart."

"I think you're perfect." She added quickly, "In a physical sense."

His grin was boyish. "When you meet my parents, you can tell them that. I'm sure it'll make my mother very happy."

"I'm going to meet your parents?" she asked, surprised.
"Of course."

She'd never given his family any thought. Introducing her to his parents was the last thing she'd expected. Their circumstances weren't exactly normal. Whatever would his parents think of their forced relationship? "Do they live on Krina?"

"Yes, in Tinara."

"I'll have to go to another planet?"

"No, it'll be a virtual visit."

"What will they think of me? Won't they mind that you've chosen a human instead of a Krinar mate?"

"Don't worry about that now. That's for the future." He brushed his knuckles over her cheek. "You never told me how your parents died."

She stilled, the familiar pain lodging into her heart. "I never told you they died."

"I read it in your file."

"You have a file on me?"

"Does it surprise you?"

"I guess not."

"Was it a long time ago?"

"Not so long."

"What happened?"

She tensed. "I don't like to talk about it."

Placing her hand, that he still held, on his chest, he wrapped an arm around her waist and held her close to his body, for once touching her in a way that had nothing to do with sex. It felt good. Too good, maybe.

He lowered his head to kiss her neck. "You can tell me," he said, his breath a warm whisper on her ear.

"Why?"

"Because I have a feeling you've never told anyone."

He was right. It wasn't only that talking brought back the painful memories, but also that her brothers, Hans, and she had left immediately after to join the Resistance. No one in the Resistance asked about anyone's background. She'd left her old life behind to live in hiding, and they'd kept to themselves. Her only remaining friend was Anita, who she'd hooked up with in secret since coming to Costa Rica, but not even Anita knew exactly how it had happened. The strange thing was she did want to tell him. She'd been carrying the weight of it for far too long, never voicing her true thoughts for the fear of doing what Hans had been doing, letting hate into her heart.

Taking a deep breath, she said, "During the Great Panic, there was violence and looting everywhere in the country. Our small town didn't escape the unrest. People panicked. There was a sudden rush for the basic necessities. Food became scarce. People killed each other for fuel and water. When our resources started running low, my parents drove to a nearby farm to try trading livestock with the farmer. They didn't know looters had already attacked the farm, killed the farmer and his family, and taken shelter in their home." She swallowed. "They fired at my parents' car. My dad managed to turn around, and they almost made it home."

"Almost?" he asked softly, pulling away to look into her eyes.

"Erik was on outlook duty. We were taking turns. He saw their car as it came up the road. They'd both been shot and lost a lot of blood. They died before an ambulance could get there."

There was genuine regret in his expression. "I'm sorry for what happened during the Great Panic. It was never meant to turn out that way."

"You knew the risks when you came to our planet." She spread her fingers over his hard chest. "You must've predicted what was going to happen, or did you simply not care?"

He gave her a tender smile. "If I could, I'd take it away from you."

She blinked, not sure what to say. While she appreciated the sweet notion, a part of her still blamed him and his kind. If not for them, her family would still be alive. She'd have gone to school and studied medicine. None of this Resistance nightmare would've happened, but it was what it was, and no amount of wishful thinking was going to change that. In the bigger scheme of things, there was less pollution and Earth had started thriving again.

His tone took on a lighter note. "Do you like the flowers?"

"That was you?"

He cocked his head. "Who else?"

"I thought... I don't know. Maybe the house."

He arched a brow. "The house?"

What did she know? She didn't know what to think anymore. "Why? What's the occasion?"

He traced a finger over her jaw. "Do I need one?"

"I don't understand."

"I wanted you to have something beautiful."

"Oh."

It was sweet. Wrong. He didn't care about her in a way a man who gave a woman flowers did. It was a human gesture he'd adopted but didn't understand or mean. It only made her feel more vulnerable. She tried to break their stare, to hide her feelings, but she couldn't look away from his eyes.

"Thank you," she whispered.

"Do you like the dress? I thought maybe you're missing your Earth styles and colors."

"It's very pretty."

He brushed a thumb over her knuckles. "But?"

"I don't have the figure for it."

"I disagree."

A flush heated her cheeks. It wasn't the compliment that warmed her, but the embarrassment at knowing how her imperfections paled in comparison to his, how her body had to look next to his, although, with every passing day some of her imperfections seem to vanish. Her skin was glowing. Her hair was shining. Her nails, which used to be brittle and break, had grown long.

"You didn't eat much," he said, scrutinizing her. "Didn't the food please you?"

"No, it did. It was thoughtful. I'm just not very hungry."

He studied her for a moment longer before saying, "How about we go for a walk?"

She sucked in a breath. "Really?"

He grinned, as if he found her amusing. "Yes, really."

"You mean," she glanced over his shoulder at the off-white barrier of the wall, "outside?"

"Yes. Outside."

"Okay," she said eagerly. "That will be nice."

His fingers tightened around hers. "The cultured gardens are pleasant at this time of the evening."

The wall opened to let them out. They took a transport pod to one of the Center gardens, which resembled a small park. Ks stared at them as they passed down the pathway, some with open hostility. Zavir didn't react, and she refused to cringe. It was too good to be somewhere other than her off-white prison. Keeping her back straight, she held onto the big K's hand, drawing strength from his silent support.

Already dark, the garden was lit with soft, green spotlights. The temperature was pleasant, much cooler than the humid heat of the jungle. How did they manage that? She made a mental note to ask Zavir. The fragrance of the flowers drifted on the air. Some of the red and yellow ones looked exotic.

"This is beautiful," she whispered.

"You've seen a Krinar garden when we visited the medical center."

"Not at night."

"I'll bring you more often," he promised.

She stopped.

He gave her a quizzical look. "Is something the matter?"

"Why *did* you bring me here?"

"You need exercise."

She didn't know what she wanted him to say, but it wasn't that.

"What is it, Liv?"

"Nothing."

"It's not nothing. You're upset."

"I'm not."

"Don't lie to me."

"Zavir, let it be. Please. It's nothing."

"No. I want to know what upset you."

She took a shaky breath. "It's the way you treat me."

He frowned. "How I treat you?"

"Like a pet. Measuring how much I eat and sleep. Punishing me. Taking me out for walks. I told you before, I have feelings."

"It's for your own good."

"Taking away my freedom is for my good?"

The line of his jaw turned hard. "We've been through this."

"Before you…" She bit her lip, searching for the right words.

"Go on," he said, his face tight.

"Before you took me, I had a job. I was useful. Independent."

"Useful?" He smiled, but the gesture had lost its warmth. "Dishing up food for Resistance fighters? Cleaning up after your brothers?"

"I was studying natural medicine before then. I worked for a homeopath."

"Redundant. Our medicine is much more advanced than anything you've studied."

"That's not the point."

His voice carried an edge. "Then get to the point."

She swallowed. "I have ambitions. I need to earn my own way."

"No. You are my responsibility. I'll take care of you."

"What do *I* do?" she cried in exasperation. "Sit in a white room and go crazy while waiting for you to come home?"

"There are things you could do. Hobbies."

"It's not the same. Don't you understand? I need a purpose in life. I need to be able to make my own decisions."

He crossed his arms. "I'll decide what's best for you."

"You can't do that. That's not how it works."

"We both know you don't make the best decisions."

"What's that supposed to mean?"

"You know exactly what I mean. Do you want me to remind you what would've happened to you in that bar had I not walked in? I'm sure you get my point. We're done talking about this." He let go of her hand, advancing on the path with large steps.

"You can't lock me up for the rest of my life," she said to his back.

He turned, his eyes narrowed. "Is that right, kitten?" A look of determined calculation washed over his features. "Watch me."

Helpless anger engulfed her. There was no talking sense into him. He didn't understand, and he never would. How could he? They were from different worlds. He could never imagine what it felt like to be in her shoes, to feel the suffocating injustice and bitter anger at having been downgraded to nothing but his pet. She had no say. No opinion.

No choice. She wanted to be anywhere but here, in his hateful presence. She wanted to run, to escape. To hide.

When he resumed his stroll, his steps faster and longer, she remained on the spot. Tears built in her eyes, but she blinked them away, staring at the tense set of his shoulders as he continued, certain she'd follow, because she didn't have a fucking choice.

Everything inside her rebelled. Something snapped. Turning in the opposite direction, she broke into a sprint. She needed to get away from him. Eventually he'd find her—there was nowhere in Lenkarda she could escape to— but she could hide, if only for a while. She could have freedom, if only for a moment, and she owed it to herself to at least try. Putting all the strength she possessed into the effort, she ran for the nearest wooded area, taking a shortcut over the grass. She glanced back over her shoulder. He'd stopped, looking at her with something she'd never seen in his eyes before. Something wild. Something predatory.

Pumping her arms and legs, she ran like a crazed animal. The arched exit was closer, almost within reach. Another few seconds. Almost there. Before she skidded through it, she looked back again, only to gasp in fright. Zavir was chasing her, and he was much faster. She could never outrun him. Glancing up and down, she went right, toward the beach, but she didn't get far.

A hand clamped down on her shoulder, breaking her momentum. She would've fallen if not for the arm that came around her waist. In a swift movement, she was lifted off her feet. Her cry echoed through the space as Zavir hauled her up like a ragdoll. His boots thumped angrily on the ground. She didn't have to look at his face to know he was furious.

She struggled in his hold, but the vice of his arms squeezed harder.

"What are you going to do?" she squeaked.

"Something you're not going to enjoy."

"Zavir, please."

"I told you not to make me chase you," he said in a dark tone. "Now stop talking."

Chapter Sixteen

Liv stood on her hands and knees on the bed, naked, as Zavir ordered. She watched him from over her back, tense and frightened. His eyes looked like two pools of smoldering coals. He was naked as well, and very imposing as he stood between her legs at the edge of the bed.

"This is going to hurt," he warned, "but you asked for it."

"Zavir." His name was a plea, even if she knew it wouldn't help.

Her thighs quivered when he ran his fingers lightly over her sex. She watched as he brought his hand to his face, inhaling, then licking her moisture clean.

"Your wetness and smell tell me you want me. Pity that little mouth of yours refuses to do the same."

"That's not true. I admitted what you wanted me to."

"Still," he tilted his head, studying her intimate parts, "you ran from me when I told you not to, when I warned you what the chase does to me. When you clearly want me."

"Wanting you and being held as your pet prisoner is not the same."

His eyes narrowed at her biting tone. "I also asked you not to test me."

"Whatever you're going to do, just get it over with."

He chuckled. "Always so brave."

When his hands cupped her ass, she pinched her eyes shut, waiting for the smack, but instead, he pulled her open wider. A moment later the heat of his tongue slipped over her folds, all the way to her clit, and higher. She clenched her globes when he neared her dark entrance. Turning her face into the mattress, she hid the heat burning on her cheeks when he flicked his tongue there, too. His fingers traced her folds and clit. Her inner muscles clenched, protesting at the emptiness. She needed him to fill her, but he only teased her for a long time. Just when she thought she couldn't take it any longer, he slid his erection between her thighs, gathering moisture from her arousal. Fingers digging into her ass cheeks, he placed his cock at her dark entrance.

"Zavir," she exclaimed, apprehension mixing with lust and a curiosity darker than she'd felt before.

He gave her no mercy as the huge head of his cock applied steady pressure on her virgin hole. Or maybe he did. Something warm and wet like pre-cum lubricated her, taking away some of the burn. It stung, though, and when he finally breached the tight ring of muscle, she dug her fingers into the blanket and moaned.

"You're going to take me in this tight little hole, kitten." His voice was guttural. "All of me."

More of the hot liquid leaked into her, first increasing the burn and then easing it. She focused on her breathing as he pushed again, sliding in what felt like at least another inch. Her breath caught on a hitch as he started to move, pushing deeper with every thrust. It was too much, too overwhelming as his cock slowly sunk into her. She knew how big he was. How thick. She'd never be able to handle all of him. She clawed at the linen and bit her cheek. When he drove home with one last thrust, she let out a gasp. His fingers were on her clit and in her pussy, not teasing this time, but wrenching hard pleasure from her. The ache turned into something else. A carnal need. It grew and grew until it consumed her, until he started to pump with shallow strokes while one hand kept her in place and the other punished her sex with brutal pleasure.

Her voice was broken, uneven. "Zavir, please." That she managed to speak at all was a wonder.

"Do I need to stop?"

"No. Please don't."

Victory sounded in his tone. "Very well."

He pulled out halfway and slammed back in. Over and over. His pace was as savage as her need, the pivoting of his hips as hard as the hammering of her heart. She was going to pass out. Needing to hold onto him, she reached behind her and gripped his wrist. His fingers were bruising her hip. His cock was bruising her inside. She was too full and too empty, but when he shoved two fingers into her sex, she convulsed and exploded. She came, stars and spots marring her vision. He pumped harder, holding her up when her knees gave out. He thrust one last time, lodging himself deeper still, and grunted out his climax. Jets of warm liquid filled her as his cock swelled and jerked. Her body had long since turned to jelly. She collapsed face down on the bed when he let go. He followed her down, kissing her nape while keeping his weight on his arms. When he pulled out, she wasn't capable of forming more than a whimper.

"I'm going to take care of you," he whispered.

A sob wracked her body and then another. Maybe it was the hard way in which he'd taken her, or the implied meaning of his words–that she'd lost her independence and freedom irrevocably–but she couldn't stop crying.

He gripped her chin and turned her face to the side. "Shh. I'll make it better." Kissing her lips softly, he ran a hand down to her hip. "Don't move."

She tensed when he lifted from the bed. "What are you going to do?"

"Relax. Your punishment is over."

She couldn't move even if she wanted to. She was boneless, aching in her core.

He returned with a glass filled with milky liquid. After helping her to sit up, he said, "Drink."

She sniffed at the liquid. "What is it?"

"It will make you feel better."

Too drained to argue, she swallowed it down in one go. It tasted sweet. Immediately, her aches vanished.

He put the glass aside and gathered her in his arms. "Let's get you cleaned up."

She leaned her head on his chest as he carried her to the shower. He held her while the intelligent shower cleaned their bodies and hair. When they were dry, he fed her a bowl of soup in bed and pulled her into his arms. She nestled against him, too tired to fight the warmth of his strong arms, until her eyes drifted closed.

"I'm not letting you go, kitten," he whispered in her hair.

"I know." She wrapped her arms around his waist. "You need to know I'll never stop trying."

"Trying what?"

"To get away."

"Go to sleep." He kissed her temple. "You need your rest."

"Zavir?"

He threaded his fingers through the strands of her hair. "Mm?"

"Tell me something beautiful."

She didn't know why, only that she needed a kind word–something pretty–to hold onto. She was so desperate, she'd even settle for a lie, as long as it was sweet.

His hand stilled. "Like what?"

"Anything that ends happily."

She waited, hoped, but there was only silence.

———

LEAVING LIV TO SLEEP, Zavir got out of bed at sunrise, dressed, and made his way to Anita and her cheren, Wian's dwelling. He pondered his problems on the way.

After what Liv had told him about the circumstances of her parents' deaths, he understood her brothers' quest with the Resistance better. They were doing what he would've done if he'd been in their shoes–avenging the death of their family. At least Liv was wise enough to see beyond the vengeance, to understand that the Krinar was here to stay, in peace, and that any fight against them was suicide. Her brothers were lucky to have her. She was a compassionate and insightful woman, a woman whose parents had been taken from her as a direct consequence of the Krinar Invasion. In her eyes, that made him the enemy, but he'd make up for it every day of the rest of their lives. In the end, after enough time had passed, surely the pain would fade, and maybe she'd be able to look at him and see more than an enemy. One thing was for sure– he couldn't let anything happen to her brothers. Learning to forgive his kind, and in affect him, for her parents' death was one thing. Not keeping his oath to save her brothers after he'd stolen her freedom in exchange would not go well for him.

Hans, Karl, and Erik seemed to have disappeared from the face of the earth. He wasn't making progress in his search for the traitor, either. A team of guardians appointed by the Council was questioning all inhabitants of Lenkarda, and all security feeds had been filtered. They'd found nothing. Every person who'd been in Lenkarda on the day of the escape was still there. No one had been allowed to leave. No reason had been given for the sudden lockdown. Only three people knew about the escape–Korum, Xita, and himself. Korum felt it was safer if less people knew, plus they were trying to avoid a pandemonium that could lead to a flare-up in Resistance attacks.

He had to consider the only logical conclusions. One, the twins and their leader were somewhere where the Krinar cameras couldn't penetrate. Two, the person who'd helped them escape was still in Lenkarda. Scanning brain memory to find the culprit was the only option left. It was a lengthy process. To scan every person's brain would take more than a month. Time was a commodity he didn't have. In less than three weeks, he'd have to hand Liv over to be used as bait in any way the Council saw fit. She'd be released with a big, fat target on her back, inviting hits from Keiths and humans alike. The Resistance wanted revenge for her betrayal. The Keiths wanted to make an example of her. Everyone wanted her dead. She wouldn't last a day. Not on her own.

Whoever freed her brothers and Hans would surely come for her, if someone else didn't get to her first. It was a mess. On top of that, her demeanor concerned him. With every passing day, the light in her eyes dimmed a little more. It was as if her fire was burning out. Since it was that very fire that first attracted him to her, he couldn't let that happen, not that he'd like or want her less, but he'd never forgive himself for breaking such a beautiful creature. Of all the things he wanted for her, crushing her spirit wasn't one of them. Why couldn't she accept her fate and just let him make her happy? He could give her anything her heart desired. Health, protection, eternal life. Wasn't that enough?

With his mind clouded, he announced himself at Wian's dwelling. A short while later, the wall disintegrated to reveal Anita standing on the threshold. Her hair was bed messy, and she still wore her sleepwear.

"This is an early surprise," she said, tying the knot of a robe around her waist.

Judging by her attire, too early. "My apology. I hope I'm not disturbing?"

"Not at all. I was just making coffee." She stood aside. "Come on in."

Wian appeared in the entrance of the lounge. At the sight of another male facing his charl, his face turned tight. With long steps, he crossed the floor to place himself in front of Anita.

He acknowledged Zavir with a nod. "What can I do for you?"

"Actually, I'm here to see your charl."

Wian crossed his arms. "What about?"

"I need to ask her a favor."

"No."

"You don't know what I'm going to ask."

"I don't need to. My charl won't do you any favors."

She pushed Wian aside. "You're being rude." To Zavir she said, "He's just being over-protective."

"I hope you are well," Zavir offered.

He didn't hold out a hand in greeting as per the human custom. It was forbidden for any man to touch another's charl, and he wasn't in the mood for having his arm ripped off.

He turned back to Wian. "Do I have your permission to speak to your charl?"

Walking toward the kitchen, she asked over her shoulder, "Would you like something to drink?"

"It seems like it," Wian said grumpily. He stood aside, letting Zavir enter.

"Juice?" Anita asked. "Or maybe an infusion? I know you don't drink coffee."

"Too much caffeine is not healthy for you," Wian said, following her to the kitchen.

"Sorry." She went on tiptoes and kissed Wian's cheek. "It's the one addiction I can't give up." She winked. "Not even for you."

Wian made a noise that sounded like a snort, but his eyes warmed with a deep glow.

"Nothing for me, thank you." Zavir took the plank she indicated. "I know your cheren is anxious for me to leave, so I'll get straight to the point."

Wian placed a protective arm around her shoulder.

She smiled. "I have to admit, I'm curious. Whatever favor could you need from me?"

"To pay a friend a visit."

"A friend?"

"Liv."

"Liv?" Her brow pleated. "Why? I mean, I don't understand. I know you were her contact with this whole Resistance thing, but what is Liv to you?"

"My charl."

She took a quick step forward. "Your what?"

"We're having an engagement party in a few weeks' time, which will double as a confirmation ceremony. I'm announcing it to the world then."

She appeared calm and collected, but there was note of hysteria to her voice. "Is this a joke?"

"Not remotely."

Fisting her hands at her sides, she took another step toward him. "Where is she?"

"Here."

She gaped at him. "Here, in Lenkarda?"

"Yes. I'm concerned about her. I think a visit from a friend will do her good."

"When did this happen? Why hasn't she come see me?"

"She's not allowed to move around freely."

"What?" she exclaimed. "Are you telling me you're keeping her prisoner?"

Anger sparked in him, but he pushed it down lest Wian threw him out before he'd gotten a commitment from Anita. "I'm keeping her safe."

Her eyes narrowed. "I see. Then I must assume your concern is as much about her wellbeing as her safety. The arrests were all over the news. I was worried sick when I couldn't get hold of her. We assumed the Council was hiding her somewhere until things cool down." Her tone held an accusation. "Little did I know."

"As I said, I think a visit from a friend will cheer her up."

She fixed that narrow-eyed look on Wian. "Did you know about this?"

"First thing I hear about it."

"Why wasn't I told?" she directed at Zavir.

"I haven't sent out a memo to every resident in Lenkarda," he said drily, "but the grapevine gossip will inevitably take care of that."

"Zavir," Wian said, his voice all but a growl, "watch your tone."

Crossing her arms, she tapped her foot on the floor. "How long has she been here?"

"Just over a week."

"You were supposed to free her and her brothers. That was the deal. That's why I told her to go to Korum."

"I don't do deals."

She opened her mouth to say more, but Wian laid a hand on her shoulder. "This isn't your fight, Anita."

"Are you letting her out at all?" she asked Zavir.

"I would, if she didn't try to run away."

"Can you blame her?"

"This is what's safest for her," Zavir said, his tempter slipping. "Maybe you can help convince her."

She shook her head. "You're unbelievable."

"Despite what you may think, I want her to be happy."

"I'll go this morning," she said, glancing at Wian, who gave her a nod.

"Thank you. I'll be indebted." Zavir got to his feet. "I won't keep you longer."

He inclined his head in greeting. At the door, he turned. "I'll expect a report."

"Don't expect me to betray my friend's trust. Whatever Liv tells me in confidence will stay between her and me."

He shrugged. "Very well. I admire your loyalty."

He'd just have to record their meeting.

———

IT WAS late morning when the entrance of the house opened. Liv jumped to her feet when Anita appeared in the opening. Rushing to her friend, she gave her a hug. "What are you doing here? How did you get in?"

"Zavir programmed access for me."

"He did? I'm surprised he even told you I'm here."

"He thought you might do with some company."

"Damn right. I'm going out of my mind. Zavir won't let me go out or see anyone. He won't even tell me how my brothers are doing." She gripped Anita's hand. "Do you have any news?"

Anita made big eyes and glanced at the ceiling.

Liv followed her gaze. "What?"

Her friend placed a finger in front of her lips.

"Oh." Of course. The house. It's telling Zavir everything. "I hate this house," Liv said heatedly. *Take that, House.* "It's not a crime asking for news, is it?"

"We haven't heard anything other than what's on the news. I asked around, but any information related to your brothers is top secret."

Liv's shoulders sagged. She slumped down on the long float, dragging Anita with her. "I just want to be sure they're all right."

"I'm sure they are, or Zavir would've told you."

"I guess."

"He seemed really concerned about you. Is he treating you all right?"

"He's feeding and clothing me, and he goes out of his way to spoil me. He gave me flowers and a pretty dress, as well as my favorite meals, books, and music. I suppose, in his own way, he tries to even show me affection."

"But?"

"But I'm his pet. His prisoner."

"Oh, Liv. That sucks. I'm so sorry."

"In three weeks' time, he's throwing an engagement party." She held out her hand, showing Anita her ring.

"Yes, he told us. That sure is a pretty ring."

"There must be something I can do, someone I can petition."

"I'm afraid that's not how it works."

Liv spread her arms. "This is my fate?"

"It's not so bad, you know. I'm very happy here."

"It's not the same. You and Wian love each other. He didn't kidnap and hold you against your will. You're free to come and go and have a job."

"Well," Anita brushed a curl behind her ear, "free to an extent. Wian is very possessive."

"Will he forbid you to see your family?"

"No, never, but our circumstances aren't the same."

"You mean your family hasn't been a threat to the Krinar rule."

"Liv, he must feel something for you if he's willing to take you as his charl."

"Oh, he does. *We* do." She brushed out the creases in her skirt, avoiding her friend's eyes. "It's called lust."

"Isn't that the beginning of love?"

"It doesn't matter. I can't live like this."

"You know what? You need to get out more."

Liv snorted. "Tell me something I don't know."

Anita sat up straighter. "You need sun and fresh air. You need out of this bubble. A swim in the ocean and a barbecue on the beach."

"Zavir will never let me."

"The men can come along. That way, Zavir can make sure for himself that you don't run away." She smiled conspiratorially. "They can take care of cooking our lunch."

"It sounds wonderful. I'd do anything for a day out of these rooms. It feels like I'm locked up in a padded asylum."

"I'll speak to Wian, so we can set a date."

"What about your job?" Anita was a children's book illustrator, and her schedule was always hectic.

Anita grinned. "One day isn't going to make a difference. Anyway, my leave is overdue."

Liv hugged her again. "You're the best."

Anita stayed for lunch, and only left when Wian called to say he was worried because it was getting late. Liv's mood was much lighter after the visit.

Zavir smiled at her when he got home. "You look happy."

"I won't exactly call it happy," she retaliated, "but I am thankful for the visit."

"You're welcome."

"I didn't say thank you."

"You implied it."

"The mere fact that I'm saying thank you for a visit from a friend should tell you how wrong this situation is."

His face drew tight. "Don't start. We've been doing great for all of a minute."

"Jeez, we're making progress."

"Liv."

The way in which he said her name made her shut her mouth. Rubbing her temples, she walked to the kitchen. Thanks to the ever-intelligent, tattletale house, there were no tasks waiting for her, but it gave her time to compose herself and find calm. Starting a fight wasn't going to help.

"Wian said Anita wants to go on a picnic."

She turned back quickly. "At the beach. What do you think?"

He crossed the floor, coming to a stop in front of her. A smile played in his gray eyes. "You seem excited about the idea."

"I am." She swallowed, waiting for his verdict.

He lowered his head, so they were on eye level. "Are you going to make a run for it again?"

Defeat and humiliation heated her cheeks. She shook her head.

"Pity." He cupped her ass, pulling her against his hard body. "I enjoyed the aftermath."

Annoyed again, she pushed away. "I didn't."

"That's the point of punishment." His smile turned knowing. "Although, you didn't hate all of it."

Why did he always have to mock her with her weakness of will? Wasn't it enough that she lost the battle? Every time. Wasn't her humiliation enough?

A stormy hue replaced the bright glint of his eyes. "What is it, Liv?"

She schooled her features, knowing her anger was showing on her face. She'd never been good at hiding her feelings. Brushing it off with a, "Nothing," she turned for the bedroom, but he grabbed her wrist.

"What just happened?"

She shrugged. "Nothing. Really. I need a shower."

"Nothing?" He scrutinized her. "The one minute you're excited about going on a picnic, and the next you look like I ripped your last bite of food from your mouth."

Counting slowly to five, she breathed in and out. "I'm sorry if my look offended you. Will you just let me go so I can have my shower?"

"You don't need one."

"How the hell do you know?"

"You had one not over an hour ago."

Was he serious? She freed her arm with a jerk. "You're an asshole."

"So, you've said."

She couldn't deal with this–*him*–right now. She tried to move around him, but he blocked her way.

"Spit it out, Liv. Why are you acting like this? Are you having your period?"

That was it. Her anger bubbled over like an ugly cauldron full of poison. She acted before thinking, striking out to hurt him as much as he was hurting her, but he caught her wrist before her palm could connect with his cheek.

His words were measured. "Be glad I caught you in time."

"Why? Because you would've given me another spanking? My, oh my. What a hypocrite you are."

"I didn't slap you in anger. That was discipline. It was different." His gaze pierced hers. "And it made you wet."

Tears welled in her eyes. She pulled on his hold, but he wouldn't give. It only fueled the tears of helplessness and anger flowing over her cheeks, but she refused to acknowledge them.

Blinking through the tears, she said, "That's exactly it."

Frustration laced his voice. "What is exactly what?"

"Why do you have to keep on rubbing it in my face?"

"Rubbing what in your face?"

"My losses. My weakness. Every fucking battle I lose. Isn't my humiliation enough for you?"

"Your humiliation?" He stared at her, his expression dark. "If I wanted to humiliate you, I guarantee you wouldn't have had an ounce of pride left in your body. And sex with me is not a battle. My bed is not a battlefield where enemies slay each other. We both come. Every time."

"You don't understand," she whispered.

"Make me, damn you."

"You can't."

"Why in all of your gods' names not?"

"We're not the same."

The minute the words were out, he stilled. They both

did. It sounded too much like a verdict. One by one, he lifted his fingers, releasing her. She took a step back and another.

When he didn't chase her, she said, "I'm going for a shower. I don't care what the house said or what you think I need."

Turning her back on him, she rushed to the bathroom, expecting him to come after her, but he didn't. Only a stunned kind of silence followed her into the space. The strained atmosphere remained as she stepped into the shower, not to clean herself, but to hide. In the privacy of the cubicle, she gave free reign to her tears, letting them fall with abundance.

———

THE SMELL of Liv's tears and the sounds of her sobs reached Zavir in the bedroom. He was tempted to go after her, but a small voice coming from somewhere other than his mind, a place closer to his heart, told him she needed her space. Space from him.

Zut.

He'd tried everything he could think of. Humans were more complicated than he'd thought. Relations with Krinar women were a lot less confusing. They got together with a male, had sex, repeatedly if they enjoyed it, and after forty-seven years, if a bond had formed, they mated. Liv enjoyed sex with him, of that he was sure. Her physical reactions couldn't lie. They did it repeatedly. A bond had definitely started forming, at least for him. The latter part scared him, but he was willing to take any consequences that came with claiming the little human as his charl. She was his. Was from the minute he'd laid eyes on her in that bar. It was too late to turn back. He knew that, but how did he make her accept it? It always came back to the same question, and he wasn't any closer to an answer than the day he'd decided to take her for himself.

The house announced a caller at the entrance, distracting him from his thoughts. Xita. Activating the hologram on the intercom, he asked impatiently, "What is it?"

"Quite a welcome," she replied in Krinar.

He switched to their language. "Cut out the sarcasm. What do you want?"

"You're no fun when you're grumpy. No wonder your charl can't live with you."

"I'm in no mood for your psychoanalysis."

"Touché. Let me in. We need to talk."

"About what?"

She glanced above her but kept quiet. Whatever she had to say, she didn't want the Krinar eyes in the sky to record it.

"This better be important," he said through tight lips.

The wall disintegrated to let Xita in. She was wearing a tight, red dress with a long slit, revealing a slender leg.

"What's with the attire?"

She cocked a hip. "Like it?"

"Does it matter?"

She gave a sultry smile. "No. I have an embassy event to attend. I thought it would show our willingness to meet our Earth partners halfway if I dress according to Earth standards."

"You're here because?"

She crossed the floor, craning her neck to see into the bedroom. "Where's your charl? I'm curious to see how she's doing."

"Get to the point."

She sighed, stopping short of him. "May I at least have a drink? It's a long trip to the embassy."

"Why don't you go by pod?"

"I'm driving with the ambassador in his limo."

He ordered refreshments from the house but didn't offer her a seat. He wanted her gone before Liv had finished her shower.

"Thank you," she said when he handed her a Krina juice.

"You're not with government affairs. Why the sudden interest in the ambassador?"

She took a small sip, barely wetting her lips. "It's on Korum's orders. Information sharing."

"Information sharing?"

"That's why I'm here. I can lose my job over this, even get exiled to Krina or have my memory wiped, but I thought you should know."

He tensed. "Know what?"

"I found something going through the memory extraction records we took of the rebels."

"What?"

"I think I know where our rebel twins and their leader may be hiding."

"Where?"

"There's a Resistance cell in South Africa that used to be run by Keiths. Your charl's brothers have visited it more than once. It would make sense that we can't trace them there. Keith technology sends any invasive or external probing devices back like a mirage. It's a kind of a safe house, for a lack of a better term."

"Why hasn't Korum informed me?"

"He thinks your charl is compromised."

"Like a double agent?" he asked with disbelief.

"Exactly."

"How does he intend to prove it?"

"By ordering a memory scan."

He balled his hands. "No."

"You won't be able to stop it. The order will come from the Council."

If guilty, Liv's memory would be erased. He'd disappear from her mind. Everything they'd shared would be gone.

"What about the brothers?" he asked tightly. "How is Korum going to deal with them?"

"He doesn't have a choice but to honor the deal you've made. The ambassador doesn't. He didn't make a deal."

"That's why Korum is sharing the information with the ambassador. He knows the South African government will send someone to take them out."

"Yes."

"Zut." Liv would never forgive him. It was the one thing that would irrevocably decide the fate of their relationship. He'd keep her, and she'd hate him forever. He'd have no chance at finding common ground or peace with her. "You have to tell me where Karl and Erik are."

"I can't say for sure they'll be there, but here, take this." She handed him a microchip reader. "It's the location."

"Thank you. I'm grateful."

She smiled. "You're welcome. See? Told you I'm on your side. There's a little bit of good news in this for you."

"What?"

"I scrambled the location. Korum is having a team on it as we speak. I'd say you have about a week before they crack the code."

"If he finds out–"

"Shh." She pressed her finger on his lips. "He's not going to find out it was me, unless you talk."

"I won't betray you. I promise."

"How are you planning on dealing with this? If you free the twins, Korum will know it's you. He'll want an explanation."

"I'll think of something."

"Just remember, my ass is on the line, too."

"I won't forget, and I won't forget what you've done for me."

Going on tiptoes, she snaked her arms around his neck. "Don't I get a little more than a thank you?"

He gripped her hips to push her away. "I appreciate what you did, but–"

Her lips covered his. Her body molded to his in a familiar way, a way he remembered well, but it was wrong. Offensive. Before he had time to break the embrace, a sharp inhale of breath came from the door. He gripped Xita hard, setting her aside roughly before turning his attention to the person who'd made that little hurtful sound.

Liv stood on the threshold, wearing one of his exercise T-shirts. Her face was paler than usual, and her eyes red-rimmed from crying. Straightening her back, she said, "I'm sorry. I didn't realize you were busy, but if you're going to fuck someone else, at least have the decency to do it somewhere different."

Chapter Seventeen

The woman Zavir held in his arms was painfully beautiful. It was Xita from the medical center. It didn't help that she was as perfect as Zavir or dressed for a ball. Liv felt small in Zavir's over-sized T-shirt, and not in a physical sense. Inwardly, she cringed.

"Oh, dear," Xita said, switching to English. "She's very catty."

Zavir responded harshly in Krinar, to which Xita snickered.

She walked over to Liv. "How are you doing? Adapting to life in Lenkarda?"

Locked up as a prisoner? Was the woman being sarcastic?

Xita sighed. "Maybe you don't know, but Zavir and I are old ... acquaintances."

"Yes," Liv said. "That was obvious."

"Well, then. I'll be off." On her way to the exit, she gave Zavir a kiss on the cheek. "Don't miss me."

Liv stared at the wall through which Xita had disappeared.

Silence stretched. Zavir seemed to be at a loss for words.

"Just so we're clear," she said, "are you a polygamous species?"

"No," he replied, his nostrils flaring, "although, it's not unheard of for a mated Krinar couple to take a charl."

"So, it's possible that you'd mate with a Krinar woman in the future and keep me as charl."

"Never. I don't share, and I don't believe in double standards."

"Ah, so fucking someone else would be cheating."

"I wasn't fucking her."

"Not yet."

He walked to her. "What's that supposed to mean?"

"Were you going to?"

His face was an unreadable mask. "No."

"Did you?"

"Did I what?"

"You know what I'm asking. Have you fucked her?"

He worked his jaw sideways, the muscles bunching. After a strained silence, he said, "Yes."

"Was it serious?"

"The attraction was mutual, that's all. It didn't last long."

"How?"

"How what?"

"How did you fuck her?"

"Liv, stop it."

"Tell me, Zavir. I want to know. Harder than me?"

"Yes," he gritted out.

"Did you hurt her?"

"No. She's a Krinar."

"She can take it. She can take what I can't."

"Where are you going with this?"

157

"Did you lock her up to fuck her?"

He fisted his hands. "No."

"Ah, she gave it to you freely."

"So do you."

"Maybe you should get a harem or something."

A spark of surprise lit his eyes. "Are you jealous?"

"Me? Jealous?" She laughed. "Why would I care?"

"You *do* care," he said, this time with a hint of satisfaction.

She blew out a puff of air. "In your dreams."

"Why can't you be honest? What are you so afraid of?"

She crossed her arms. "Nothing."

He cupped her cheek, his tone turning soft. "You're the only woman I want, kitten."

"Really?" She nearly bit her tongue for how hopeful it sounded. "Why should I believe you?"

"Because I won't lie about this."

"I trusted you once and look where that has gotten me."

"You know why I shot your brothers and took you. I've already explained why I'm keeping you."

"Yeah. To fuck me while you keep me safe. Oh, and you like having an amusing pet around."

"I'm not going to fight about this any longer. I have my reasons for what I did, and if you were objective for once, you'll see I'm right." He brushed a thumb over her cheek. "All I ask is that you trust my intentions, if not my word. Everything I do is for your safety. I don't want to harm you, little kitten. I just want to keep you. Is that such a crime?"

She hung on his words, her gaze stuck to the movement of his lips. Her heart had paused on the promise underlying those soft-spoken words. Could she trust him again? Could she trust his intentions?

For the first time since they'd met, vulnerability flashed in his eyes. There was a side to the big, dangerous man she didn't know, a side she'd glimpsed in the little things he'd done to make her life beautiful and easier.

"All right," she said, letting out a slow breath. "I'll try to trust you again if you work to earn it."

He nodded. "Good. Now, if I remember correctly, this conversation started about a picnic."

"Yes," she agreed, albeit a bit less enthusiastic than before. All these intense emotions were draining. Maybe she *was* going to have her period.

He smiled. "I have urgent business to take care of, but I can put it off for a day. I know this is important to you."

It was a sweet gesture, one of those things that made her like him more than a little and gave her hope. Could she be more than his amusement? Did she *want* to be more? She averted her gaze, not wanting him to see the conflict in her eyes. "Thank you."

"I'll let Wian know."

"Okay," she said placidly. "Can I call Anita? We'll need to discuss what to prepare for lunch."

"Call whenever you want."

She bit her lip, staring at him from under her lashes. "Thanks."

"You're welcome."

He placed a kiss on the top of her head, and then he was gone.

She didn't waste time. She requested the house to call Anita and sighed with relief when her friend's face appeared in a holographic image.

"Oh, thank God," Liv exclaimed. "I thought Zavir would never let me talk to anyone else."

"He just called Wian. We're on for tomorrow."

"What do we prepare?"

Anita laughed. "I knew it would cheer you up. I'll take care of the food. Just bring your bikini."

A thought struck her. "I don't have one."

"I'm sure Zavir will take care of it for you."

"I suppose so, but it bothers me that I can't take care of it myself."

"Things will change. Just wait and see."

After discussing the lunch menu, Anita said goodbye to catch up with work. Liv went to bed with the tablet, trying to focus on reading, but nothing interested her. It was already late when she commanded the lights off, and still Zavir hadn't returned. Lying in the dark, she couldn't help but mull over their discussion. For all her intentions to trust him, she also couldn't help but doubt. For all she knew, he was with Xita.

Stop it, Liv.

Those kinds of thoughts weren't helping. Zavir had been right about one thing. She was jealous. She was jealous *and* envious. Too much was at stake to be honest, even with herself. Her pride had taken a knock and her body had been punished, but what she was afraid of was having her heart trampled.

———

AFTER SPENDING the night going through every bit of information he could find on the safe house, Zavir returned home to pick up his charl for their date. A real date, this time, even if it was a double date. He was eager to get to the Resistance safe house, which was on the other side of the globe, but he had a week before Korum's team cracked the code, and Liv was more important. She hadn't been as excited about anything since the fried chicken substitute in the bar.

Indeed, her eyes were glittering like blue gemstones when he walked through the entrance.

"I'm ready," she announced, standing in the lounge wearing a sundress with thin straps and no bra, looking gorgeous, soft, beautiful, and like everything he wanted.

His gaze dropped to the hard tips of her breasts. "You're not going like that."

"What do you have against topless tanning? I do it all the time."

Imagining her semi-naked on a beach with other males, his vision went dark and just a bit red at the edges.

She came closer, flashing him a teasing smile. "What's the matter?"

His hunger for her grew to a dangerous level. He ordered both his dick and the possessive beast in him down, fisting his hands not to grab her. "Why do you think something's the matter?"

She stopped flush against him. "You look kind of murderous right now."

"What can I say?" He studied her face, enjoying her smile. "I'm possessive."

"Don't worry." She took an elastic band from her wrist and tied her hair into a ponytail. "I'm only joking, but if you don't want me swimming naked, I'll need a bathing suit."

"Already taken care of." He held out the parcel he'd brought.

"I didn't know there was a bathing suit shop in Lenkarda."

"There isn't. I made it with nanotechnology."

She took the two-piece from the bag, holding it up in the air.

"Really?" She flushed a little as she said it.

"What?" It was white with silver chains for straps.

According to the data, it was made to the latest Earth fashion. "Don't you like it?"

"It's beautiful. Stunning." The red color of her cheeks deepened. "It's just…"

"Just what?"

"I'm not sure I have the body for this."

"Your body is perfect. Just how I like it. You'll look beautiful. Perhaps too much. On second thought, maybe I should make you something less revealing, like a surf suit with a high neck and long sleeves. The sun *is* harsh out here, and your skin is very fair."

She had the nerve to roll her eyes. "I know the nanocytes you pumped into me will heal any sunburn and prevent skin cancer. We're already running late. I'll put this on, and we can go."

"Yes, kitten," he said obediently, resisting the urge to slap her ass, or pull her dress over her head and do other things that would make them even later.

When she exited from the bedroom wearing the bikini under her dress, he had to adjust his hard-on.

"Come on," she said. "I don't want to make them wait."

Smiling at her enthusiasm, he took her hand and led her to the pathway that gave access to the beach. It was a beautiful day with a cloudless sky. Anita and Wian were already waiting under the palm trees on the white sand. A picnic table and chairs had been set up, as well as a portable barbecue.

"Very Earth style," Zavir said as he took everything in.

"Men here on Earth love to grill stuff on the barbecue," Anita said. "I'm sure it will grow on you."

While Liv helped Anita set the table, he discreetly scouted the area, making sure there was no danger. After a lunch of grilled peppers stuffed with minced mushrooms and herbs, and some Krina vegetable varieties on the side, Liv pulled her dress over her head.

She dumped it on a towel spread out in the sun. "Let's go for a swim."

His mouth went dry. The bikini showed off her enticing curves, and even if he'd seen those curves plenty of times naked, he'd never seen them in three scraps of material that hinted, hid, and in the process teased. She was already walking to the water when he was finally able to move again. He caught up quickly, taking her hand to lead her into the water. There were many dangers in the sea—creatures that stung, coral that cut, currents that swept away.

They swam out a long way into the sea, until the turquoise water turned dark blue.

"That's far enough," he said.

She splashed water at him. "Scared?"

She had no idea. The fear of losing her was a fear bigger than any he'd faced in his life. What was he to make of it? He wasn't sure he liked the feeling, but it was what it was. It came with the choice he'd made.

"I'm tired," she said. "I'm going back."

Silently, he swam next to her, matching her strokes, making sure he could catch her if her arms grew tired, but she was a strong swimmer, stronger than most.

"Did you train for swimming?" he asked as they exited the water.

She caught her ponytail and squeezed the water out. "It was part of my military training."

He stopped. "Military training?"

"My brothers wanted me to be able to fight if needed."

Taking her hand, he led her over the sand toward their picnic spot. "What else did you learn?"

"How to fight with a knife. How to fire just about any

gun or rifle."

"I don't like the sound of it. It's dangerous."

"They didn't give me a choice." She pulled on his hand, bringing him to a stop again. "Will you?"

He contemplated his answer for a while. How was he supposed to put it without causing another argument, without raising another barrier?

"Let's go for a walk," he said.

They took a path that led into the jungle and curved along the shore.

"It's beautiful here," she said, looking around. "Peaceful."

He pulled her into the shade of a tree. "I have to go away tomorrow."

Alarm filtered into her eyes. "Where?"

"I can't say."

She leaned against the trunk, her gaze wide on him. "You're going on a mission."

"Kind of."

"Zavir…" Biting her lip, she glanced down at where she dragged her toe through the sand.

He gripped her chin to turn her face back to him. "Are you worried about me?"

She gave him a crooked smile. "Kind of."

Warmth glowed deep in his chest. "Playing word games with me?"

"Of course not. You don't play games."

"No, I don't." He trailed his hand down the curve of her neck, cupping her nape. "You remember well."

"When will you be back?"

"As soon as I can. The house will provide for you. If you need anything while I'm gone, you only have to ask."

"You're going to keep me locked in while you're gone?"

His chest tightened, a bit of the earlier warmth evaporating. "Why do you ask when you know the answer?"

"What if… What if you don't come back?"

"I'm not planning on getting killed."

She studied him with her big, troubled eyes. "No one ever does."

"I'll come home to you, kitten. That's a promise."

She nodded, suddenly very interested in her toes again. He waited, feeling more coming.

When she faced him again, her eyes were more sad than clouded. "You didn't answer my question."

"Which one?" he asked, knowing exactly, but putting off answering. He could only answer truthfully, and she wasn't going to like the truth.

Her voice was soft. "Will you ever give me a choice?"

Dragging his hand to her shoulder, he absently caressed the spot where he'd bitten her. She already knew the answer to that question, too. It was best to approach the answer differently. "If I do, will you stay?"

Her eyes started to shimmer as she stared up at him. The seconds ticked on as she considered the question. Like him, she seemed reluctant to give him anything but the truth, but it wasn't always easy telling the truth. The truth, if yes, could set her free, or no could confine her to her prison. The fact that it took her so long to speak already told him the nature of her truth. It squeezed his chest harder and twisted his insides, even as he felt the tears that started dripping from her eyes as if they were his own. They continued to stare at each other, the unspoken a weight between them.

Finally, she whispered in a pained tone, "I honestly don't know."

It slayed him, those words, in ways he couldn't explain or understand. He wanted her, but by zut, not at this price. It never occurred to him how his feelings, this unknown devastation raging through him, would come into the equation.

Wiping away a tear, he kissed the wet skin of her cheek. "Will it be so bad, staying with me?"

His words only made her cry more. She sobbed so hard she couldn't speak.

Taking her in his arms, he held her against his chest. "It's all right. You don't have to answer."

All he could do was hold her until the worst of the storm had passed.

Somewhat calmer, she pushed away from him, rubbing the heels of her palms over her eyes. "I'm sorry. I don't know what's gotten into me."

He wanted her more than anything, but he cared too much to see her like this. "Liv, I–"

A female voice called from the path. "Thank goodness. There you are."

Anita and Wian came rushing up to them. The looks on their faces promised nothing good.

Anita grabbed Liv's hand. "We just got some news. It's about your brothers."

Liv paled. "What's happened?"

"They escaped."

Zut.

"What?" Liv looked between Anita and Wian with huge eyes. "When?"

"The day after they were brought here, as far as we can tell."

Liv's gaze turned to Zavir, her eyes burning on him. "Did you know?"

"Where did you get the information?" Zavir asked Anita. "It's classified."

Wian replied, "Someone at the memory bank leaked the info to the media. By now, the whole world knows."

Liv stood straight, her hands fisted and her body shaking. She seemed to be seeing nothing and no one other than Zavir. "You asked for my trust."

In front of Anita and Wian, he adopted a stoic face, but inside he was unraveling. "I couldn't tell you."

"There's more," Anita said. "There's a price on their heads. They've just become the most wanted men in history."

"From who?" Zavir gritted out.

"Government law enforcement agencies. The twins are wanted for multiple crimes, including treason and possession of illegal arms."

"I can't believe this." Liv wiped her hands over her face. "This wasn't supposed to happen. It's all my fault."

"I'm sorry," Anita said. "I know how much you love your brothers."

"There'll be no saving them now," Wian added regretfully.

"If you don't mind," Liv said, "I'd rather go."

"Of course." Anita gave her a sympathetic look. "I understand. I'm sorry you had to find out like this."

"I appreciate you telling me." With a cutting look at Zavir, she headed down the path.

"Liv." He went after her, taking her arm. "Let me explain."

She pulled free from his hold, not slowing her stride. "You lied to me. Again."

"I didn't tell you, but I didn't lie."

"It's the same damn thing," she said over her shoulder.

Zavir could only stare after her, defeated and doomed.

"This time," Wian said as they watched her go, "you really screwed up."

"Why do you say that?" Zavir snapped.

"If you ever had a chance with her, you just blew it."

Chapter Eighteen

Liv's insides shook with worry, disappointment, and anger when Zavir let her into his quarters, but she kept her lips sealed. If she opened her mouth, she was going to say things she'd regret. How could he keep this information from her, thinking it would never get out?

Much as on the beach, they stood facing each other silently, but with a very different ambience. She waited for his explanation, but all he said was, "I'll be back as soon as I can."

That was it?

He attempted to smile, but it was a weak effort. "Don't you have anything to say to me before I go?"

What else did he expect her to say? Thank you for betraying her trust? Again?

He nodded slowly, as if the absence of her words gave him insight into her thoughts. "The truth is I care about you." He traced her jaw with a finger, as if memorizing the lines of her face. "Take care, kitten." His cocky smile returned in all its glory. "Try to behave."

She bit back a retort, feeling the loss of his touch as

profoundly as a dip in temperature when he dropped his hand. Yes, there was much to say, but her wounded pride wouldn't let her. Her battered heart fluttered as he walked away from her, and her throat throbbed with suppressed tears when he exited into the jungle and the wall closed on his disappearing shape.

"Be safe," she whispered to the hole he'd left, feeling the loneliness all the way to her soul.

———

WHAT WAS he going to do when he found Liv's brothers and their leader? Zavir considered his options. He'd honor his promise to Liv. He'd send them back to Lenkarda for their memory deletion before someone else found and killed them, and life would go on. Without Liv. The thought ripped his heart out, but he'd rather go through his days an unhappy bastard than having her tears. That was what she wanted. Freedom. It had been on the tip of his tongue to grant her wish before Anita had interrupted them. He rubbed at the aching spot in his chest. Was this what the bond felt like? Like your insides were minced and you couldn't do anything but stand by and let it be trampled because the happiness of someone else was more important than your shriveling life? That life stretched out in front of him, eternal and colorless. After Liv, everything would seem bland. Only one thing was left—the only thing he knew. Fighting.

Pushing the door to Korum's invention lab open, he passed through the scanners and reported at reception. After clearing the unscheduled visit with Korum, the receptionist showed him to Korum's office without delay. The Council member didn't look happy.

"It's on the news," Korum said.

"I know."

"I can't give you the month you asked for. Public relations are too explosive."

"I'm aware of that, too. I'm here to offer a deal."

Korum raised a brow. "You? A deal? That'll be a first."

"I'll find your Keith. I'll hand him over before the end of the week in exchange for Liv's freedom."

Korum crossed his arms behind his back, studying Zavir with a contemplative look. "You'll denounce her as your charl?"

"I want you to guarantee her safety and that you'll let her walk free if I give you our traitor."

"You realize she'll have to stay here in Lenkarda or go to Krina?"

"Yes." With her new immortality, they couldn't send her back into her own world. He understood that.

"Another Krinar may take her as charl."

"Yes." He clenched his jaw so hard it felt like snapping. "I'm aware." The day that happened, he'd be moving to another galaxy. He wouldn't be able to witness Liv in the arms of another man. He'd rather die.

"What about her brothers and their leader?"

"I'll deliver them for memory deletion and rehabilitation as originally agreed. No harm is to come to them."

"The Council won't like it."

"It's the same as our original agreement, except there's an added bonus. Now, you'll also get your traitor."

"You seem sure of finding him."

"I am."

"What new information do you have?"

"I have a lead to follow up."

"I want to know everything you do, down to the minutest detail."

"You will, in time, but for now I have to ask you to trust me."

"You ask a lot."

"As you said, I'm sure of finding the Keith. If I bring down the traitor, I want his identity to be revealed." He couldn't help his bitter tone. "The public must know the truth. If they know Liv wasn't involved in the escape, that she's not a *double agent*, it will take the target off her back, enough for her to be released without her life being in danger."

The Keith would be captured and the last of the Resistance squashed, eliminating that danger, and Krinar would know for sure she was on their side.

"You want me to release her?"

"In a day's time."

"She'll go when you bring me my traitor, not a day before."

"Fair enough. With one condition. If I don't return, you will see to it yourself that she's freed and safe."

Korum wiped a hand over his jaw. "You drive a hard bargain."

"It's my first and only bargain." He smiled wryly. "I have to make it count."

"Fine," Korum said slowly. "Your team saved my life when Saret tried to get me killed in the arena. I haven't forgotten. You have a deal."

Zavir nodded curtly. "Thank you. I'll report back in a day's time."

In the bay area, he created a pod and programmed his destination. The quicker he could get to South Africa, the quicker he could find Hans and the twins, interrogate them, and find out who was working for them on the inside.

———

THE HOUSE CONNECTED Liv to Anita, but she had no news from Zavir or where he was headed. Neither did Wian. Wherever he'd gone, it was secret. Of course, it was. He was heading into another fight, and she was trapped here, worried sick. About him. About Karl and Erik. She couldn't stand it any longer. She hated being kept in the dark.

Absorbed in her worries, she jumped when the entrance opened to let Xita into the room.

"What are you doing here?" Liv asked.

Xita gave her a sugary smile. "Good day to you, too."

"I mean, did Zavir let you in?"

"No. I stole the access code."

"You did what?"

"That's why I came over the other day." She held up her hand, flashing a silver ring. "Stole the code with this while he was ordering me a drink."

"With a ring?"

"It can copy the codes from his personal house computer." She waved a hand. "It's complicated."

"Why? What do you want?"

"It's your lucky day. I'm your knight in shining armor."

"My what?"

"Isn't that how you say on Earth? I'm here to help you escape."

Chapter Nineteen

"Where are you taking me?" Liv asked.

She sat next to Xita in a pod, flying in invisible mode low over the sea. After Xita had erased the trackers in Liv's body, she'd taken her to the hidden pod and manipulated the technology that tracked every departure from and arrival into Lenkarda. This way, their escape wouldn't be on the radar. No one would know until it was too late.

Xita adjusted the controls. "As I said, to your brothers."

When Xita had said she was there to help Liv escape, Liv had hesitated, knowing the extent of Zavir's wrath and worried he'd come after her. Only after Xita had told her she'd be taking her to her brothers did she agree.

Liv's heart started beating faster. "Where are they?"

"At your safe house in Johannesburg."

"I've never been to a safe house in Johannesburg."

"Your brothers have, when they first met with the Resistance. It's run by Keiths, although, after the last attack there aren't many Keiths left. The place is deserted now."

"How did they get there? How did they manage to escape?"

Xita flashed her a smile. "How do you think?"

"You helped them like you're helping me."

"Right answer."

"Why?"

Xita's smile turned broader. "I have my reasons."

"What about their memories?"

"The holiday idea didn't work. There were too many inconsistencies. It was an interesting experiment, but a failure."

Liv winced at the experiment part, as if her brothers were nothing more than test subjects.

"Anyway," Xita continued, "if I was going to help them escape, they needed their full memories, which is why I reversed the process before it became permanent."

Even if she was grateful for the escape and her brothers' memories, Liv didn't trust the woman's intentions. She had nothing concrete to base her judgment on, except for a feeling in her gut that told her Zavir was at the crux of Xita's motivation.

"You want me away from Zavir," Liv said. "Is that it?"

"Does it matter why I did it? You're out of Lenkarda. Isn't that what you wanted?"

Yes, that was what she'd wanted, but the idea of Xita with Zavir didn't sit right with her. She couldn't stomach the notion, never mind conjure the image. It was more than just jealousy talking, because her heart hadn't stopped aching since Zavir left.

"Do you have news from him?" Liv asked carefully.

"I sent him on a–How do you say?–wild goose chase. I gave him a false location of the safe house."

"Why would you do that?"

"I needed to create a diversion to get you alone. It was the quickest way to get Zavir to leave." Seatbelts appeared from the thin air, snapping around their upper bodies. "Hold on. The next part is going to be fast."

"Wait a minute. What if he finds—?"

Her words were cut off when the pod shot forward, pushing her back into her seat. Light exploded around them in rainbow shards as they zipped through the sky. It was only when the pod descended a few minutes later that Liv could lift her hands from where she'd gripped the armrests.

"Sorry about the rough ride," Xita said. "The pod is outdated, but at least no one back in Lenkarda will miss it."

"Why didn't you just make one?"

"I don't have a powerful enough fabricator. It's not a tool required for my occupation."

Liv looked around. They'd landed on what seemed like an abandoned industrial site surrounded by vast fields.

"This is it?"

Their safety belts drifted away. "Come on. Your brothers are waiting."

They made their way inside the building. Plaster and brick rubble littered the floor. Through a gap where a wall used to be, two silos were visible. It had to have been a flour or seed plant. Graffiti marred the walls. They trudged over the debris and climbed a flight of stairs. The upstairs level consisted of a single space, like a huge warehouse or office floor. Three-quarters of the walls were missing. Only the pillars kept the roof up. Sunlight filtered in from three sides. In a far corner, under the shady protection of the peeling ceiling, stood a desk with several monitors on it. Behind it, stood two men.

Liv's breath caught. She rushed forward, happy tears filling her eyes. "Erik! Karl!" Embracing first the one, then the other, she stood back to take them in. They seemed healthy. Normal. Not like they'd been shot, and their minds tampered with. "Are you all right?"

Karl's face softened. "The more important question is how are you?"

"I'm fine." She wiped at the tears on her cheek. "Great, actually, now that I'm seeing you. I was worried sick."

Xita reached them, stopping with her hands on her hips. "A happy reunion, I'd say."

"Thank you," Liv whispered. "Thanks for bringing me here."

"The pleasure is all mine."

Liv gripped Karl's hands. "How long have you been hiding out here?"

"Since Xita brought us."

"What about your memory? Your gunshot? How do you feel?"

"The gunshots were treated with nano-healers," Erik replied. "We remember everything. There's nothing to be concerned about."

Thank God for that. Xita hadn't lied. She glanced around. "Where's Hans?" Her throat tightened as she asked the question. Could she face him? Could she forgive him?

"I'm here," a voice said from behind.

She twirled to see a figure emerging from the shadows. Hans. He was as tall and imposing as ever, dressed in his military combat attire. She studied his face as he entered the light. His eyes were harder. Colder.

"Well, well." He barely disguised his sneer with a smile.

"Look who's here. If it isn't the Krinar's informant. Or shall I say pet? It seems you forgot your leash and collar."

Liv pulled back her arm and swung her fist. Hans ducked to the left but was too late to escape the blow. The full force hit him on the nose. Cartilage crunched. Blood spattered.

He stumbled a step sideways before righting himself, touching his nose. When he brought his bloodstained fingers to the light, his expression turned thunderous.

"You bitch."

As Hans reached for her, Karl grabbed his arm, holding him back. "You deserved that."

"And this." Liv pulled back again, put her full weight into the momentum, and planted her fist in Hans' stomach, just like Erik had taught her.

Hans bent over, wheezing. Xita chuckled.

"That was for calling me a pet," Liv said.

Hans went for her again, but Erik grabbed his other arm. "That's enough. Calm down, Hans."

He jerked free, his hateful eyes on her. Gripping his nose, he forced it straight. "You broke my fucking nose."

"That," Liv said, putting her face in his, "was for torturing me."

He gave her a frosty, half-smile. "You deserved more than you got."

"If Zavir hadn't showed up, I would've been dead."

"You should've been."

"Hans," Erik said with a warning in his voice. "I said that's enough."

Erik was right. They didn't have time to waste. "We need to talk about what we're going to do." Every Krinar and Earth law enforcement organization would be looking for them, not to mention Zavir.

"I think you've had enough fun," Xita said, aiming a weapon at Liv.

Liv took a step back, her heart slamming into her ribs.

"What are you doing?" Karl exclaimed. "She's one of us."

"No." Xita's finger tightened on the trigger. "She's one of them."

Chapter Twenty

L iv woke in semi-darkness. Her body ached, and she couldn't feel her left arm. She was lying on her side, trapping it under the weight of her body. Rolling onto her back, she managed to free it. Life came back with pins and needles. She was alive. There was enough light filtering through a high window to recognize Erik and Karl lying next to her. They weren't tied up.

She scrambled onto her knees. "Karl," she whispered, slapping his cheek. "Wake up."

He mumbled a protest before jack-knifing into a sitting position. "Where are we?"

"I don't know."

Judging from the graffiti on the walls, they were still in the factory.

She crawled to Erik and shook his shoulder. "We have to get out of here."

"What happened?" Erik asked grumpily, getting up onto his elbows.

"Xita darted us," Karl said. "I don't know what she's up to, but Hans is in on it."

Erik's tone was bitter. "We've been betrayed."

Getting to her feet, Liv felt the door handle. The door was locked. She judged the distance to the window. It was too high to reach, even if they stood on each other's shoulders. The walls were too smooth to find a grip.

"I think we're in one of the silos," she said.

A sound came from the other side of the wall, like metal scraping over metal, and then the door opened. She rushed forward, her brothers close behind, but a security gate blocked the exit. Xita and Hans stood on the other side.

She gripped the bars. "What are you doing?"

"Haven't you figured it out?" Xita asked.

"Zavir will find us."

"Oh, he will, but first, he'll pay handsomely to have his precious little pet back."

"You're doing this for money?" Karl bit out.

"You, too, Hans?" Erik asked, his eyes accusing.

"Zavir will bring the ransom in exchange for Liv," Hans said, "but when he comes, we'll be ready for him."

"It's a trap," Liv exclaimed.

"Of course." Xita shrugged as if the admission carried no significance.

"Why?" Liv forced through dry lips. "I thought you wanted him for yourself."

"The only thing I want from Zavir," Xita said, "is his head on a spike."

Liv's heart twisted. Her insides went cold. "What can you possibly gain from killing him?"

"Hans wants the money." Xita crossed her arms. "I want the power."

"I don't understand," Liv said.

Xita brought her face closer to the bars. "Do you know

what it feels like to always be overlooked, to always have someone else promoted above you? I've done everything the Council has asked of me better than anyone, but did they turn to me when it was time to announce our presence on Earth? No, they trusted the task to Korum. Korum," she spat.

"You're a scientist," Liv pointed out.

"I'm a strategist. I've been one longer than Korum has been an inventor, until they decided my strategy for Earth was of no use to them."

Karl pushed forward. "Your strategy?"

"Get rid of the weak," Hans said, "and keep the strong."

"This is what you believe?" Erik asked, sounding incredulous. "This is what we've been fighting for?"

"Look around you." Hans said. "The weak are dragging the rest of us down. We want to start a new colony where sick and poor won't exist."

"What exactly are your plans for this so-called colony?" Karl asked.

"We want our own government and our own laws," Xita said. "We've already established how Earth should be divided."

"Let me guess," Erik said wryly. "You get to be the ruler."

Xita smiled. "Exactly."

"What does that make you, Hans?" Erik asked. "Her lapdog?"

Hans pointed through the bars. "Shut up or get your teeth kicked out."

"He's second-in-command," Xita said. "I make the rules, and he's there to make sure they get executed."

Liv shook her head. "If you divide the Earth, some people will be separated from their families. We're living in a global world. You can't just draw a line from east to west."

"That's exactly what we intend to do," Xita replied.

"How are you going to weed out the weak?" Karl looked between Xita and Hans. "Kill them off?"

"Everyone gets a fair chance," she answered.

"What's that supposed to mean? You're going to hold gladiator games?"

"Not quite. The Krinar have always been hunters. I'm one of many who believe we should go back to our natural state, to the way nature intended us to be. Our laws will allow hunting. It'll be a natural way of superior selection. Only the strongest will survive, as always in nature. Ignoring this fundamental law by nurturing the weak and sick will only upset the balance of evolution and lead to overbreeding."

"This is truly what you believe?" Liv asked Hans, unable to process the words.

"This is my vision, yes."

"You do realize it'll be a mass genocide of the human race?" Erik asked. "Eventually, you'll end up like everyone else, as prey."

"Not if a Krinar adopts me as charl."

"That's your way out?" Karl asked in disbelief. "To hide behind the skirts of a woman?"

"It won't be hiding," Hans said. "It's called survival."

Karl looked pointedly at Xita. "I assume you've already found your sponsor."

"When did this happen?" Erik asked. "When did the two of you conspire?"

"Since the beginning," Hans said. "Everything was going according to plan to take over Lenkarda and over-throw the Council, but then Liv came along and screwed it all up."

"In the end she did us a favor," Xita said. "This way will be quicker."

"Zavir is a guardian," Liv said. "He's loyal to his people. He'll never give in to your demands."

"When Zavir learns we're keeping you hostage, he'll do anything to get you back, even put himself at risk. He'll sacrifice himself if he believes it will save you."

The blood left Liv's head, making her feel dizzy. "How is killing him supposed to help you?"

"As part of the ransom, he's going to provide us with the codes for bringing down Lenkarda's protective shield. With Krina's best guardian and Resistance hunter out of the way, we'll take every Krinar, charl, and Council member in Lenkarda hostage and no one will go free until the Council agrees to our demands."

"They'll never."

"They won't have a choice. It's either that or have every inhabitant of Lenkarda tortured to death."

"They'll come at you with everything they've got," Erik said.

"It'll be too late. We have the technology to set up borders around our territory that not even the Krinar can infiltrate, thanks to my brilliant research."

"You mean you stole it from the memory banks of your scientists," Liv said wryly.

"Korum not only developed the perfect weapon to destroy the shield, but also a new, stronger shield. He demonstrated it when he melted half of Saret's lab. It wasn't hard to steal the technology. All I had to do was plant a little bug under the skin of someone who works in the Rolert lab. We know how to create the new shield. What we don't know is how to destroy the existing one. That information Korum keeps to himself. After Zavir gets the codes and we kill him, Lenkarda will not only be exposed, but also unprotected."

"You'll never get away with it."

"Let me worry about that. First things first. I'm calling Zavir, telling him what we need in return for you–enough money to fund our new government and the codes to expose Lenkarda."

"Is that where you come in?" Karl asked Hans, his face contorted with contempt. "You're doing her dirty work?"

"Call it what you want," Hans said, "but at least I'll be breathing when you're long dead."

"Each man for himself," Erik said. "Is that it?"

"That's one way of looking at it."

"What were we?" Karl asked. "Insurance in case you couldn't get Liv? Or are you going to hand us over to our authorities for a handsome reward?"

"The reward is nowhere near what Zavir will bring us," Hans replied. "You were just the bait to get Liv here."

"You don't care about the millions of people who'll be killed?" Karl asked.

"I have news for you, Comrade Karl. The Krinar have no intention of letting us live. Why do you think they came here? Their planet is dying. This is where they're going to settle, and we're an inferior species. We're in their way. This is the only way we can ensure at least some of mankind's survival."

"You don't know that," Liv cried. "They're making progress with pollution, cleaning up our mess. They want to live in peace with us, just as most humans want to live in peace with them. They have more advanced medicine and resources. They can help us."

"Such an idealist." Xita called up a hologram from her wristwatch device. "Time to tell Zavir he's been sent on a wild goose chase." She chuckled. "I do love your silly

Earthling expressions." She turned to Hans. "Lock the door. We have work to do."

"No!" Liv shook the bars. "Listen to me, please. I promise—"

The door shut with a bang in her face.

Chapter Twenty-One

The coordinates Xita had provided were wrong. Zavir slammed his hand on the control float of his pod. He was in the middle of a field of maize, surrounded by cows. Impatiently, he called up a hologram, but it was intercepted by an incoming image from Xita. Just the person he was looking for.

His words were measured. "What game are you playing?"

She smirked. "Are you enjoying the view?"

He leaned toward her image. "I won't ask again."

"You won't have to. I have your pet and her brothers."

"You what?"

"I want money and information in exchange for them."

He clenched his fist so hard his knuckles made a cracking sound. "You're going to die."

"Save the threats, Zav. The clock is ticking. You have until sunset, Earth time. I sent you an encrypted message with my demands."

The feed went dead.

His heart went colder than moonstone. His rage was the kind that frosted the blood in his veins, more dangerous than the kind that made it boil. More calculated. More deadly. Shutting down all emotions, he went into killing mode. Xita was going to pay. If there was a scratch on Liv's body, Xita would die a slow and humiliating death in the arena. It looked like he'd just found their traitor. How could he not have seen it? How could he have been so blind? What was Xita's plan with this? What could she want with money, a commodity the Krinar didn't care for, and what kind of information?

He pulled up the message the traitor had sent. If he weren't already frozen to his core, what he read would've chilled him. The amount of money she wanted was huge, but it was nothing compared to the information. The information would give her Lenkarda on a silver platter. She'd have power over everyone and everything in the Costa Rican Krinar Center. Korum, their most promising inventor and fast-rising Council member who many put their hope on for the future, was there right now, as was his charl, Mia.

Turning the pod around, he went back into the direction he came from. If he was to save Liv, he only had one choice.

————

LIV TURNED in a circle in the confines of their prison, her head tilted toward the ceiling. "There has to be a way out." All she wanted was to be back with Zavir in his safe, comfortable dwelling. She'd give anything to feel his strong arms around her.

Karl shook his head where he sat on the floor, his knees pulled up and his back resting against the wall. "You're wasting your time. You were right. We're in one of the silos. The only way out is through the door."

"Think," she urged. "If you weren't bound by the laws of physics, how would you get out?"

"Through the window," Erik said. He sat against the opposite wall, his face grim. "We'd defy gravity and float right up."

Karl's expression was despondent. "Well, we can't fly, and we're not weightless."

"We owe you an apology." Erik lifted his gaze to hers. "Nothing I can say or do will ever take away what you went through, but I want you to know I'll regret it for the rest of my life. Hans said he wouldn't hurt you, and we were stupid enough to believe him. We trusted him. We fought not only for our freedom, but also to avenge Mom and Dad's deaths. If we weren't so blinded by our vengeance, maybe we would've seen the truth."

She blew out a long breath. "You took a stance for your beliefs. You did what you believed was right."

"We should've listened to you."

"He's right," Karl added. "We failed you. We failed in the promise we made to Mom and Dad."

"Not yet," she said. "It's not too late until the end. We have to keep on fighting."

"She's right." Karl pushed to his feet. "We can't give up."

She looked between her brothers. "If we can't get out, we need a plan."

"You're both missing the most obvious way out of here," Erik said quietly.

Karl gave him a skeptical look. "Which is?"

"Through the door."

"It's locked," Karl pointed out.

"Until they unlock it."

Karl frowned. "What's your point?"

"At some stage," Erik continued, "they have to open the door."

"In case you haven't noticed, there's a security gate."

"One of them has the key."

Karl shrugged. "So? They're still on the other side of the gate."

"We have to make them come inside," Liv said as she grasped Erik's meaning.

"We have to get into a fight." Erik nodded at Karl. "If it gets violent enough, someone has to come in and break it up."

"You're not hitting each other," Liv said sternly.

"Do you have a better idea?" Karl asked.

"Let me think."

"No time." Erik took a wide stance. "You start, Karl. I'm ready."

"This is madness," Liv cried, but Karl's fist was already swooshing through the air, hooking under Erik's jaw.

The force of the blow made him stumble back. He'd scarcely regained his balance when he lowered his head and charged. His head connected with Karl's stomach, knocking Karl to his knees.

"Stop!" Liv banged on the door. "You're going to kill each other."

A trickle of blood ran from Erik's nose. Karl was doubled over. Erik was about to charge again when the bolt sounded on the outside of the door. It swung open, letting in a stream of daylight. Hans stood in front of the gate, a gun with a silencer screwed to the barrel in his hand.

He pointed it through the bars at Liv. "Cut it out or I shoot her in the leg."

She sucked in a breath, but at least her brothers stilled.

Karl pointed at Erik. "He started it."

Erik wiped the blood from his nose. "He asked for it."

In a flash, Erik was behind her, one hand around her neck and the other bending her arm behind her back. He held her body like a shield in front of him. No matter how good a shooter Hans was, there was no way he could fire a shot without the risk of hitting her.

"It's her you want," Erik said. "We were just the bait to get her here."

Karl moved behind Erik. "Let us go, or he breaks your trump card's neck."

Hans' nostrils flared. He flicked off the safety clip.

"If she's harmed," Erik said, "Zavir won't be giving you a damn thing, and you know it."

"Let us go, and you can have her."

Hans sneered. "No deal. You're bluffing."

"You think I won't do it?" Erik laughed softly, applying pressure on her windpipe.

She gasped for air, clawing at his arm with her free hand, but Erik was much too strong for her to fight.

"Stop it," Hans gritted out, panic showing in his eyes.

"Not until you let us out."

She kicked, her vision already starting to go blurry.

"Last chance," Erik said, his voice taunting.

Hans uttered a curse and glanced over his shoulder. "Xita!"

The second was all Karl needed. He charged. Before Hans could register what was happening, Karl planted his boot on the hand that aimed the gun through the bars. Caught between two bars, the force snapped Hans' wrist with a sickening crack. The gun clattered on the ground. Hans uttered a scream, falling to his knees, cradling his arm.

At the same time Karl snatched up the gun, Erik let

her go. She sucked in air, gasping like a drowning person. A shot went off, the sound muffled by the silencer. Everything was happening too fast. Karl grabbed Hans' collar through the bars before his body could fall back.

"Help me," he said over his shoulder to Erik.

Still catching her breath, she could only look on as Karl held Hans up while Erik went through his pockets.

"Hurry up," Karl said, pointing the gun at the outside.

A jingling sounded, and then Erik produced a set of keys. "Got it."

She closed her eyes, sinking to her heels. Her throat was on fire on the inside. She desperately needed a sip of water.

"Come." Erik was back at her side, helping her up. "We've got to go."

She forced her legs to obey while Erik unlocked the gate and Karl kept watch with the gun. When they climbed over Hans' body, she couldn't contain a shiver. His hand was twisted at a strange angle and bone stuck through the skin.

"Don't look," Erik said, pushing her forward. "Just move."

Karl went out ahead, pointing the gun left and right as he scanned the floor. They were on another level. So far, there was no sight of Xita.

Just as Liv let out a tremulous breath, Xita's voice sounded from the stairs. "What's taking so long, Hans?"

The sound of her shoes echoed off the concrete as Erik dragged Liv behind a cluster of barrels and pushed her head down. From between a gap in the drums, Liv watched with a stammering heart as first Xita's shoes and then her legs became visible. She walked onto the floor, her expression one of irritation. Her eyes narrowed when she spotted Hans' body and the open door.

Liv closed her eyes and prayed. When she opened them again, Xita was turning in a slow circle, taking in the space.

"You can come out," Xita said. "I'm not upset. In fact, you did me a favor. I was going to get rid of him anyway."

"Don't move," Erik hissed softly in her ear.

Xita went to Hans's body and kicked it over, obviously looking for the gun. She peered inside the room and flicked a finger over the keys still hanging in the slot.

"Here, kitty," Xita called in a mocking tone. "Zavir won't be happy if I don't have his pet."

At the sound of his name, Liv sucked in a breath, but Erik squeezed her arm in warning.

Xita started across the floor, making straight for the barrels. "You know I'm going to find you."

One, two, three more steps, and Xita was almost on top of them. What was Karl waiting for? Why didn't he shoot? Another step and Xita's forehead appeared over the rim of the barrel. Oh, dear God. They weren't a match for the Krinar woman. She'd rip their heads clean off without even breaking into a sweat. The moment Xita's eyes became visible, Karl fired. From where he aimed, the bullet was supposed to hit her between the eyes, an instant death shot, but she ducked, faster than the bullet left the barrel. Instead of taking her out, it merely grazed her ear.

Karl fired, again and again, but the Krinar was too quick, dodging left and right. One bullet hit Xita in the arm, and another in the leg. The rest hit the drums she jumped behind for cover.

"Fuck," Karl said.

The gun was empty. Liv didn't have to look to know. She'd counted the shots. Xita rose to her feet, her face like thunder. The K's body would heal, but at least the wounds would slow her down.

Erik yanked Liv to her feet. "Run!"

They turned for the broken wall, running with everything they had. From the edge, the ground was visible two stories below, covered with a heap of burlap bags.

"Jump!"

Karl was already projecting himself through the air, aiming for the bags. Erik followed suit. She paused at the edge. They couldn't outrun a Krinar, not even a wounded one. They didn't stand a chance.

"Jump!" Erik and Karl shouted in unison, waving for her to follow.

Taking a deep breath, she turned. Erik and Karl's voices reached her from below.

"Fuck."

"Liv."

"Go," she cried without looking back. "You stand a better chance without me."

"Liv, no!"

"Go, Erik, damn you. Now."

A predatory smile curved Xita's lips. The bullet popped from the hole in her arm, hitting the concrete with a ping. The skin had already started to knit together. She advanced slowly.

Another curse sounded from below, and then footsteps hit the ground hard, moving in the direction of the fields.

"So sweet," Xita said, "sacrificing your life for your brothers'."

"It's me you want."

Xita laughed. "Stupid, stupid, girl."

Liv measured the distance. It was still too far for Xita to jump. Karl and Erik should have a good head start by now. Flinging her body to the left, she ran for the stairs, pushing down drums to create obstacles as she went. She dared a glance as she sprinted up the steps. Xita was jumping the drums like hurdles, but her injured leg made her slower and less powerful, causing her to jump short, slip, and fall over one of the drums. On the next level, Liv ran for the far wall. She'd noticed a service chute from the floor below, a pipe that had to have been used for sending bags of flour down. She was halfway there when the floor exploded behind her, bricks and plaster flying everywhere. Xita jumped through the opening, landing on her feet. Shit. She'd broken a hole through the ceiling. Refusing to give in to her fear, Liv pushed herself harder, diving the last meter through the air. She went head first into the pipe. Her body shot down like an arrow with her arms trapped at her sides, taking down cobwebs as she went. Dust made her cough.

A furious cry tore through the air. The pipe started shaking. Xita! She was breaking the pipe from the wall. Liv's body hit the small mountain of sacks just as the pipe snapped behind her. Buried from the impact, she crawled from the pile, rolling off the side to the ground. The earth shook somewhere farther. She didn't need to look to know Xita had jumped. Propelling herself forward as fast as she could, she headed for the train tracks at the side of the site where rusted containers and old train freight cars were parked. If she could reach it, she could hide. If nothing else, it would win her some time, enough to catch her breath.

Exhausted, she ran between two rows of containers until she spotted a dumpster. She threw the lid back and cringed at the bang it made. Several rats scurried out from the remains of rotting grains. She shrieked, jumping to the side. Xita was close. Liv could tell from the noise the Krinar woman made as she ripped open containers in her search. This was her only chance. It was now or never.

Chapter Twenty-Two

The new location wasn't anywhere near the original one Xita had sent. This one was outside a town called Johannesburg. Zavir had wasted too much time already with Xita's misleading directions. Xita wouldn't harm Liv until she'd gotten what she wanted. That was the knowledge he held onto to keep it together, to not lose his mind.

The surroundings became clear. His navigation system announced he'd arrived at his destination. Two silos dominated the dilapidated scene. From the outside, it falsely appeared as if there was no life within. The shield surrounding the area bounced back any heat and energy search rays. It required an enormous amount of energy, energy that could only be pulled from the antimatter in the void above. The hole in the ozone layer just above their location made it easier to pull the antimatter down before transforming it into shield energy. The isolated area was a perfect hideout for a few rebels.

His senses on high alert, he scanned the building. Liv was close. He could feel it. Logic told him to move toward the abandoned structure, but his gut told him otherwise. Following that little voice some called the bond, he moved soundlessly toward the tracks littered with broken containers and old train freight cars. The closer he came to the silos, the stronger the bond grew. The containers gave way to what used to be a loading dock. Then he stopped dead. Xita stood in front of one of the bins, her arm stuck elbow-deep in its foul-smelling content.

"Xita."

She flung around.

He widened his stance. Every word was articulated, a warning. "Where is my charl?"

She extracted her arm speedily, shaking morsels of grain from it. "Where are my goods?"

"My charl first."

She walked to him with a swagger. "You'll get her when I see what gifts you're bearing."

She was bluffing. He knew her too well. It was in the way she'd said it, her voice an octave too high.

She stopped in front of him. "Did you come unarmed?"

"And alone, as you instructed."

She checked her wristwatch device, no doubt to monitor the airways for pods or concealed flying bots. "Let's see it."

"First my charl," he said, biting off each word.

"I could kill you and just take the codes and ransom money."

"You could, but that would slow you down considerably, seeing that I memorized the defense codes, and the money transfer will only be initialized once I see Liv and her brothers, without as much as a scratch on their bodies."

She tilted her head toward the bin. "She's in there."

"What?" Was this some kind of joke?

The look on Xita's face told him no. With two long steps he was at the bin, peering inside. It was big enough to house a human in a sitting position, but no human would be able to breathe under that mass of rotting grains. With a fury born from panic, he gripped the sides and tilted the bin, emptying the contents on the ground. A few rats scrambled from the bottom, but other than that, there was nothing but decay.

His fury turned to full-blown rage. Turning slowly, he fixed his gaze on Xita like a missile locking onto a target. He was going to take her apart, limb by limb.

Her eyes grew large. She was surprised. She'd seriously expected Liv to be at the bottom of that goddamn filthy bin.

He took two steps toward her. "Where is she?"

She cocked a hip, keeping up the act of bravado. "Here."

Another step. "Here, where?"

"In the tower."

His gaze slipped to the twin cylinders. "You're lying."

"She's somewhere here. Let's play a game of hide and seek."

"You don't know where she is. By zut, you lost her." But he couldn't be one hundred percent sure.

"You walk, and I say hot or cold. That's how the Earth game works."

He grabbed her neck, squeezing hard. "I'm going to kill you."

"There's a room on the first floor. I locked them in there."

He searched her eyes, but this time she was telling the truth. Her pupils didn't dilate, neither did her irises darken in the way they did when she told a lie. He let go. There wasn't a minute to waste. Turning on his heel, he hurried toward the building.

He almost felt the weapon she turned on his back at the same time she spoke.

"You know I can extract the codes for the defense fields from your brain."

He flung around, coming face to face with a laser gun. "Not if I'm dead."

"The brain is an amazing thing. It acts as a storage device, just like a computer. It's a mirror of your memory. Even if you're dead, I can simulate brainwaves to make your brain think it's alive, and it will give me everything I want to know."

"You failed before you started, Xita. You never stood a chance. Did you really think I'd steal the information and risk the life of every person in Lenkarda?"

Her cheeks darkened. "You would, for your human mate."

He smiled. "There's been no public announcement, and there was never going to be. She's not my human mate. She's a pet, nothing more, and pets are replaceable."

Her nostrils quivered. "You lie."

"I'm rather fond of Liv, and I'd like her back, but not at the price you suggested. I'm afraid you made too much of my affection for the human girl. The sex with her is good, but at some point, it always gets boring. Don't you think?"

"If not to retrieve her, why did you come?"

"Why do you think?"

"You think you're going to kill me?" She uttered a cynical laugh. "I've been around for much longer than you, long enough to know real love when I see it."

"I've already told you–"

She pressed the nozzle against his temple. "Liv! Come

out or I kill him."

His breathing quickened when he realized her plan. "You're mistaken. Liv doesn't care about me."

"Oh, what a stupid male you are. Of course, she does. She'll prove it in the next few seconds, too."

"Leave the human out of this. It's between you and me, now. This is our fight."

"I'm going to kill her," she said so softly he had to strain his ears to hear, "right here, in front of your eyes. If she's not your human mate as you claim, you shouldn't mind too much."

"You can kill both of us, but I still don't have what you want. I could never give it to you."

"You came here on a rescue mission. You wouldn't have come with nothing."

"The only reason I'm here is because the Council sent me on a mission to capture you."

"Then you would've done so by now."

"It would've been nice to have the humans alive, but I'll live with the collateral damage."

Her gaze filled with hatred. "No one is going to stop me. Not any longer. Not you or the Council." Her finger hovered on the trigger button. "I'm going to do it the Earth way, Liv. I'll count to three, and then he's dead. One."

"No, please."

The familiar voice shook him to his core. No. She wouldn't do this. Liv wouldn't sacrifice her life for his.

They both looked up to where the voice had come from. Liv was climbing down the ladder mounted on the side of the cylinder nearest to them.

"That's where you were hiding." Xita snickered. "No wonder I couldn't pick up your smell. You were above the wind. Clever."

"Stay there," he called.

"I'll kill him," Xita warned.

Liv's feet hit the ground.

"Don't you dare, Liv," he said through gnashed teeth.

"Let him go," Liv said. "You can trade me for what you want. My government will give you the money, enough to bribe someone else in Lenkarda for the information."

"She *does* love you," Xita said with cruel satisfaction. "Pity you don't feel the same about her. Come here, Liv, and I'll let him go."

Liv approached, tears streaking her cheeks. His heart broke with every step she gave. This wasn't the plan. The plan was to convince Xita Liv meant nothing to him. He hadn't bargained on Xita turning his own plan against him. He should've known she was cleverer.

"You're going to give me the codes," Xita said to Zavir, "and I'll make her death quick. We're going to test them together, and you better hope they're authentic, or the human loses a finger for every false digit. She'll die slowly."

Liv's throat moved as she swallowed. "You said you'd let him go."

"Did I? I must've lied."

Liv's gaze widened. "Krinar don't lie, not about killing."

"Oops." Xita shrugged. "I must be the exception. Time's up." She held out a palm to Zavir. "Hand it over."

He noticed the movement from the corner of his eye. Liv did, too, because her lips parted on an inaudible gasp. A look passed between them, a quiet understanding, and when Erik brought down the pipe, Liv and Zavir ducked. The blow hit Xita on the crown of her head. Karl aimed for the back of her legs. Her knees buckled, the weapon going off before she'd hit the ground. Instead of tearing through the wall, the laser beam hit a piece of broken mirror that lay among the rubble on the ground.

It happened too fast for Liv to register the danger, but Zavir had time to drag her down, covering her body with his.

The beam hit the mirror and ricocheted back at an angle, the full blow of it hitting Xita in the chest. Her body jerked. The weapon dropped from her hand. She fell over backward, her eyes like two, dull black marbles in her skull.

"Oh, my God." Liv reached for her. "Get your nano-healer. Quick!"

Zavir gripped her wrist, holding her back. "Don't touch her. It's too late. She's charred on the inside. Her brain is fried."

Erik and Karl dropped their pipes, breathing hard.

Zavir got to his feet, cradling Liv under his arm. The danger wasn't over. "Where's Hans?"

"Dead," Erik replied.

"It's a long story," Karl said. "I suggest we get out of here. We'll fill you in on the way."

He hugged Liv tighter, unable to deal with how close he'd come to losing her. Her body shook from shock. His hands were all over her, not only soothing her, but also reassuring himself that she was alive. Unharmed. He needed to get her out of here.

"Let's get to my pod," he said, lifting her in his arms. "There's a lot of explaining to do."

Liv tensed in his hold. "My brothers." She looked at Karl and Erik. "You have to go. Run. You'll be arrested. Both our government secret service and the Krina Council are looking for you."

Erik shook his head. "We're not leaving you again."

"I have nothing to hide," Karl said. "Everyone needs to know the truth."

Chapter Twenty-Three

S tanding in Zavir's quarters, Liv took in the familiar setting with gratitude. Everything was the same, except for the extra bedroom and en-suite bathroom where Erik and Karl were getting cleaned up, and the exterior walls that were now transparent from the inside instead of off-white.

She was freshly showered and dressed, waiting for Zavir to finish his turn. He'd neither chastised her for escaping with Xita, nor touched her since they'd gotten back. She was a nervous wreck, anticipating his wrath, and worse, his punishment. Or maybe he'd meant what he'd said to Xita, that there was never going to be an announcement party because she was expendable.

Warm hands on her shoulders startled her. She flung around. Zavir was dressed in the typical off-white, casual Krinar attire. The fabric of the sleeveless shirt stretched over his chest, defining his powerful frame and exposing his huge arms. The drawstring pants sat low on his narrow hips. It was strange not to see him in combat clothes.

He studied her with a pained expression. "Why are you standing here, staring at nothing?"

"You changed the walls."

"It's always been like this. I gave them a solid appearance when I first brought you here because I thought you wouldn't appreciate feeling exposed until you got used to … things."

Things. That small, non-specific word that held so much meaning still stood between them.

"You added a room."

"I had Wian modify it for me when I knew your brothers would be coming home with us."

"That fast, huh?"

"A fabri–"

"Fabricator, yes I know." She tried to smile, but the strain sounded in her voice. "It's nice. I like it."

He touched a finger to her face, gently tracing the line of her jaw. "What were you thinking about?"

"I never thought I'd be so relieved to be back," she confessed.

His face tensed. He withdrew his touch. "If you ever put yourself in danger like you did back there, there'll be hell to pay. You'll never do something so foolish again. Understand?"

"She was going to kill you."

"I asked if you understand."

She lifted her chin to meet his gaze. "Yes."

His gray eyes turned a shade darker. "Good."

She hugged herself. "Are you going to punish me?"

He reeled at her words. "For what?"

"For escaping."

"Give me your hand."

Reluctantly, she placed her hand in his.

"Come." The wall disintegrated to let them out. "I want to show you something."

"What about Erik and Karl?"

"We won't be long."

They took a transport pod to the medical center. Taking a path through the front garden, they followed it to the building. Krinar and a few humans stared at them as they passed, but there were none of the earlier hostility.

She gave Zavir a sidelong glance. "Do they know?"

"Everyone knows."

"Erik and Karl?"

"Xita lied. She told them we were going to wipe out the human race."

"As a ploy to overthrow the current rule and establish her own colony."

"Exactly."

"She used Hans to help her achieve her plan."

"You've all been deceived."

"What will happen to my brothers?"

"They've been granted amnesty. They're no longer on the most-wanted list. On the contrary, they're being portrayed as heroes in the media for saving my life."

She breathed out in relief. "Thank God."

He squeezed her hand. "So are you."

She looked up at him quickly. "Me? Whatever for?"

Bringing her fingers to his mouth, he brushed his lips over her knuckles. "Do you really need to ask?"

She stopped, holding him back. "Zavir, I…" This was hard to say, especially not knowing where she stood with him, but he deserved the truth. "What Xita said is true. I do love you." She'd realized it in that awful moment when Xita had pressed a laser gun to his head. She'd rather die than let anything happen to him.

His face transformed into a strange expression. It was a mixture of tenderness and regret. "I know, kitten."

Why was he looking at her like that, like he was going to say goodbye?

"You do?" she asked softly.

"A man doesn't get a declaration stronger than what you gave."

"Oh."

He pulled on her hand. "Come on. We'll be late."

"For what?"

"You'll see."

At the medical center, he let her inside first. A Krinar woman with a white overcoat waited for them.

"This is Rize," Zavir said. "She heads up the student program."

"I'm very pleased to meet you, Liv. Zavir told me you're interested in joining our program."

"What?" She stared at Zavir.

"You did say medicine was your interest, didn't you?"

"You mean, studying here?" She motioned around. "At the K Center?"

He gave her a gentle smile. "If you'd like. The Council already approved it."

"Really?" She looked back at Rize. "Are you sure? I'd hate to impose just because…"

"Just because?" Zavir prompted.

"Just because you insisted."

"Not at all," Rize said. "We'll be happy to have you. There's a lot to learn and much work, but Zavir assured me you're a bright, capable young woman. Besides, after what I've seen about you in the media, I have no doubt you'll be an asset to any team."

She beamed. "Oh, my God. I don't know what to say. Thank you so much." She turned to Zavir. "Thank you."

"You're welcome."

"When do I start?"

"Is tomorrow too soon?" Rize asked Zavir.

A closed-off look came into his eyes, but his smile stayed intact. "Maybe give it a couple of days. She's been through an ordeal."

"Of course. There's no–" Rize started saying.

"Tomorrow's fine," she interjected.

For once, Zavir didn't argue.

They spoke for another few minutes about the program, and how the training was customized for each student. The more Liv heard, the more she grew excited. This was exactly what she believed in, focusing on each student's natural strengths while developing weaknesses without forcing conformity. Rize explained how the Krinar sought to add value to their world while dabbling in many different areas, some never specializing in anything. The focus was on a qualitative, shared participation of skills, and development at each person's individual capacity. She'd be one of the very few privileged humans who'd have an opportunity to learn from the Krinar.

By the time they got back outside, her heart was a confused maelstrom of gratitude, excitement, and dread, because there was still that odd look in Zavir's eyes. They walked side by side through the garden, Zavir clearly preoccupied. In a quiet corner, he pulled her into the shade of a tree with branches that reached the ground. Covered with purple flowers that smelled sweet, they formed a heavy curtain. Hummingbirds were gathering nectar from the flowers. Their wings made a pleasant buzzing sound. It was like being in a natural dome made of flowers and birds, but the wonder of it was dampened by the doom on Zavir's face.

"Liv…" He searched her eyes. "There's a reason I arranged for you to join the study program."

She had to admit, it had come as a huge surprise. "I was going to ask."

He inhaled and exhaled slowly. "You can't leave Lenkarda."

What was he getting at? "Yes, I know."

"You're like us, now. You're not going to age like a human. It's not something we can broadcast to the rest of the world."

Biting her lip, she decided to bring up the difficult subject still tainting the air between them. "Can I travel?" she asked hopefully. "Will I be allowed to visit my brothers?"

"Yes."

Her pulse quickened. It sounded too good to be true. "I'm no longer a prisoner?"

Sadness swept over his handsome features. "No."

He didn't seem happy. Did he still prefer to lock her in after everything that had happened? Didn't he know she'd never run again?

"Zavir, I–"

"Shh." He pressed two fingers on her lips. "Let me finish. This is hard for me to say."

That feeling of doom that emanated from him started to seep into her heart. She leaned against the trunk, not sure her legs would hold her weight for what he had to say.

Framing her face with his palms, he stared deep into her eyes. "This is how it all started." He smiled, but it wasn't a joyful gesture. "Against a tree."

She couldn't stand the tension any longer. "Just say it."

Taking her hand, he wiggled the ring from her finger.

"What are you doing?" she cried softly, staring at him in confusion.

His fist closed around the ring so hard his knuckles turned white. He hardly ever blinked, but he did so now. Taking a deep breath, he dropped his hands at his sides and took a step away from her. "I'm letting you go."

The words were shards of glass in her heart. "You are?"

"You're free."

"I'm no longer your charl?"

His voice turned hard. "There'll be no party, no announcement."

Tears blurred her vision. Her chest shrunk, becoming too small to contain her heart. "What you told Xita is true, then."

He frowned. "What?" His eyes flared. "No."

She swallowed, needing a moment to find her composure. "Then I don't understand."

"I'm letting you go because I love you too much to keep you. It's what you wanted, isn't it? Your freedom."

Her heart stilled. For a moment there was nothing but the knowledge, and then it started beating again. Happier.

"I can't give you the freedom you knew before," he continued, "as you're an immortal now. You'll stay here, and…" He seemed to wrestle with the words before forcing them out. "And another Krinar can take you as charl."

"You love me," she whispered.

He bowed his head, but his strong shoulders remained proud. His smile still had that nostalgic sadness to it, but a hint of the cockiness she'd gotten used to slipped in. "How did you guess?"

"A woman doesn't get a declaration stronger than the one you just gave."

"You were right. I'm a devil. I knew from the first moment I saw you I was going to keep you. All I ever wanted was to protect you–you know that, right?–but what Korum said is true."

"Korum?"

"He said you've proven you're capable of taking care of yourself, and that I'm an overprotective, possessive, obnoxious, and jealous male."

"Yes," she reached up to cup his face. "You're all that." She smiled through her tears. "And he's a good one to talk."

Gripping her fingers, he moved her hand away. His tone turned urgent. "I'm giving you this one chance only. Run, Liv. Get away from me."

She shook her head.

"What are you waiting for, kitten? Go."

"No."

He seemed torn, confused. "What do you mean, no?"

"I choose to stay."

"Here? At Lenkarda?"

"Wherever you're staying."

"Liv, what are you saying?"

"I want to be with you, Zavir, because I choose to be. If you'll still have me, I want to be your charl, your lover, however you'll have me."

A spectrum of emotions flickered through his eyes. "Do you mean that?"

"I've never meant anything more."

Grabbing her in his arms, he crushed her to his chest. "If you choose to be mine," he said in a raw voice, "I'll never let you go. You have to understand that."

"I won't let you go, either. You're mine."

"You're right." He pulled away to look at her. "From the very start."

She held out her palm. "You have something that belongs to me."

Putting her at arm's length, he shook his head.

"Zavir?" Didn't he want her to wear his ring?

Without breaking their gaze, he went down on one knee.

"Oh, my God." She covered her mouth, staring at the beautiful, dangerous man who was kneeling at her feet, his eyes like an open book with affection written in them for everyone to see.

"Liv Madsen, will you please do me the honor of accepting this ring?"

"Oh, my God." It was the most beautiful moment of her life. No, scrap that. She couldn't choose. Every moment with him was beautiful.

"Liv?" he said, reminding her he was waiting for her answer.

"Yes," she breathed. "Oh, my God. Yes."

His face glowed with the satisfied male possession she'd come to associate with her K. "Give me your hand."

She held out her trembling fingers.

Gently, he pushed the ring over her ring finger. "There." He studied her hand, seeming mighty pleased with himself. "That's better." When he looked back at her, his expression was more intense than she'd ever seen. "Liv Madsen, will you do me the honor of being my charl?"

"Yes," she whispered. "Yes, Zavir. Nothing will make me happier."

Something like relief washed over his features, as if she'd turn him down. Getting to his feet, he drew her to his chest. "This," he said, brushing his lips over her ear, "is the most beautiful gift you could ever give me."

She went on tiptoes to put her arms around his neck and pull his head down to hers. Their lips collided in a desperate and hungry kiss. His growl made the little birds fly up in the air. Her moan replaced the humming of their wings as he gripped her hair to tilt her head to the side. His tongue was warm on her skin, his mouth searing on her neck as he kissed a path to her shoulder and back. The gentleness of his kisses contrasted with the firm hold he kept on her hair. His free hand found the curve of her breast, stroking softly.

Flicking his thumb over her nipple, he pulled back to gauge her reaction. What he saw in her eyes had to have pleased him. He rewarded her with the most tender of kisses while his breathing turned harsh and his hands frantic as he let go of her hair to flip up her skirt and move her underwear aside. She was dazed, intoxicated by his touch, only barely registering that he was lifting her leg around his waist.

"I need you," she said into the kiss.

"I know." He nipped her bottom lip. "I'll make it better."

A ripping noise sounded, and then the head of his cock nudged at her folds. She opened her eyes to look at him. His face was ruggedly handsome, his expression raw. Intertwining their fingers, he pressed her palms against the trunk above her head, reading her with intense concentration as he slowly penetrated her.

His breath whispered over her lips. "I love watching your face when I take you."

"Then watch."

He chuckled. "Always such a brave girl." He pressed deeper. "I intend to."

She gasped when he slid all the way in. A few thrusts, and she was falling apart. Her need was fierce.

"Give me what I want, kitten."

"What do you want?"

"Your pleasure. Your screams. You."

She fought not to let her head fall back, letting him see

what he was doing to her when he started to move. She didn't care that they were in a garden, protected by mere flowers and leaves. He tilted his hips, changing the angle of his penetration. The pleasure he demanded from her started to build. It was near. It was so intense it was frightening.

"Too much," she cried on a whisper.

"Everything you feel, I feel, too." He accentuated the declaration with a roll of his hips. "It's the same for me, Liv."

He let go of her hands to weave his fingers through her hair. He dragged her closer for a kiss, burning her with his lips at the same time as a fire detonated in her lower body. The orgasm crippled her, rendering her knees weak, but she wasn't the only one. His climax ripped through him, and for the briefest of moments, there was a slight tremor to the big, powerful guardian's legs.

Burying his head in her neck, he caught his breath.

Not ready to let him go, she wrapped her arms around his waist, holding him close and inside her. She wanted him to tell her this was real and not a fantasy or hopeful dream.

"Tell me something beautiful," she whispered.

"I love you, kitten."

A happy purr resonated from the depths of her chest. Was there anything more perfect he could say?

Epilogue

T he crowd hadn't dispersed yet when Liv and Zavir exited the tent in which they'd celebrated his victory. She brushed the gravel from her knees, embarrassed to think the spectators knew what they'd been doing. Applause sounded from the arena. She was still too stressed to rejoice. She'd thought she'd die when a rival for the position of Protector had insulted and challenged Zavir for a fight. The fight had been gruesome, but at least the rival lived. She was glad Zavir hadn't killed him, even if she feared how this would influence their future working relationship among the guardians.

Zavir brought her hand to his mouth. His look was possessive as he planted a tender kiss in her palm. "You're mine, Liv."

"I am." Her chest felt so light from relief she could drift to heaven. "In fact, I think I've always been."

"You *think*?" he teased. "I may have to challenge that tonight until it's a deep-sated knowledge."

Some of the spectators came up to congratulate him, cutting his suggestive banter short. Zavir had been very positive about the outcome of the challenge, insisting they celebrate their engagement party after the fight, where he planned to introduce her as his charl to the world. Even now, as Korum placed a palm on his shoulder in greeting, Zavir's dark eyes gleamed with a little of the savageness left over from the violent battle. Mia said something sympathetic about understanding what Liv had been going through. It was overwhelming, and she was grateful for Zavir's strong grip on her hand.

When they once more advanced to the floating hall where the reception was about to take place, Anita rushed up to them, pushing Ks and humans out of her way. "Wow, look at you. You look so happy." She looked Zavir over. "You both do."

"We are." Liv meant it with all her soul. She knew Zavir felt the same. They were so in touch with each other's feelings. He said it was the bond.

"Now that the last of the Resistance members who were part of Xita's cell have been detained," Anita said, "I suppose you'll be home more often, Zavir."

His eyes danced as he glanced at Liv. "That's the plan."

"There's word Mia and Korum are leaving for Krina."

"They are?" Liv looked at her cheren.

"I don't know why," Wian said, "but I have a feeling things are about to change."

"Change how?" Liv asked.

"It's not common knowledge," Anita replied, "but Mia is taking her family to Krina to meet the Elders."

This was huge. Every K and charl knew the Elders never met with anyone. Maybe, just maybe, there was still hope for all mankind.

Alir, the leader of the guardians, stepped forward to offer his congratulations. "I don't want to darken the mood of such a special event, but I thought you'd like to know that we found Juan, the man who'd betrayed Liv."

Next to her, Zavir tensed. "Where is he?"

Alir's gaze was hard. "Dead. The body was dumped in the jungle."

Liv shivered.

Zavir pulled her closer. "What happened?"

"A friend said the last time he saw him he was going to claim a reward for information on a traitor in the Resistance. We pulled the information from a Resistance fighter's memory at the memory bank. He never made it out of the Resistance camp. The minute he left their leaders' office, a soldier was waiting. He slit his throat."

Liv clamped a hand over her mouth. She still couldn't believe this of Hans, who'd grown up in her town, in her street.

"Good," Zavir said. "At least I don't have to hunt him down and kill him."

"Zavir," Liv said on a gasp.

He kissed her lips. "No more talk about this. Today is a day for celebrating only."

He nodded at Alir, who said a few more words of praise about Zavir's excellent defreb moves before excusing himself.

"Come." Zavir pulled on her hand. "There's someone I'd like you to meet before the party starts."

They went ahead of their guests to the hall that was decorated in Krina style with shimmering walls, hovering floats, exotic flowers, and a transparent floor. In the middle, a table of honor was set. Zavir led her to a plank and seated her before placing a virtual reality node on her temple. In a flash, they were standing in front of a Krinar dwelling. She could tell from the heat and strange vegetation they weren't in Lenkarda.

She looked up at Zavir. "Where are we?"

"This is my parents' house."

"On Krina?" she exclaimed.

His smile was indulgent, as if he found her reaction amusing. "Yes, kitten."

When he moved forward, she held him back. "Wait. I'm not sure I'm ready for this."

He raised a brow.

"What if they don't like me?" she asked nervously.

He gave her a chaste kiss. "There's nothing not to like. Trust me."

"How will we communicate? I don't speak Krinar."

His smile turned into a grin, as if he knew she was stalling for time. "I implanted a *chip*."

Her cheeks grew warm at the crude, non-tech description he was using to remind her of their first meeting. At least she had the presence of mind to act agitated. "When?"

He bowed low, letting his wicked smile brush her lips. "When you were passed out last night after I bit you."

"Oh." The heat in her face intensified when she recalled how loud she'd been screaming. Thank goodness the Lenkarda dwellings were far apart. Although, with the Krinar's enhanced hearing one never knew. No, best not go there.

"Come." He gave her hand a gentle tug.

The wall disintegrated as they approached. A stunning woman with black hair and a man who had a strong resemblance to Zavir waited inside. As they entered, the woman gave her a broad smile.

"You must be Liv. Welcome. We're delighted to finally meet you. I'm Vilna, and this is Arman."

The man inclined his head in greeting.

Liv could indeed understand them. It was foreign and

exhilarating, putting her slightly off-balance, but she soon discovered that Zavir's parents were kind and accommodating, going out of their way to put her at ease. Her tenseness evaporated, and before long she was enjoying an animated conversation about Krinar medicine and life in Lenkarda.

"I'm truly happy for the two of you," Vilna said after some time had passed, brushing her knuckles over Liv's cheek. "I hope you'll visit us soon again."

"I'd love that," Liv said, meaning it. Vilna was gentle and caring, and Arman had an unexpected and very pleasing dry sense of humor.

After saying their greetings and taking their leave, they were back at their float in the great hall, which was now filled with human and Krinar guests.

Karl and Erik came up to them.

"Thanks for the invitation," Karl said, pressing a palm on Zavir's shoulder.

"Thank you for coming," Zavir said, taking Liv's hand under the float.

Erik followed suit in the traditional greeting. "Wouldn't have missed it for the world." He looked at Liv's white dress. "You look gorgeous. Happy. Like you deserve."

"Thank you." She was nervous, knowing many Krinar on Krina were watching the event, like they'd been watching the fight in the arena. Both Zavir and his parents had a high standing in the Krinar society, hence many attended. She wasn't sure she liked being in the spotlight, especially since some journalists had also been invited to cover the event. Tomorrow, the fact that she–previously a member of one of the largest Resistance cells, turned informant–accepted becoming Zavir's charl would be big news.

When her brothers had taken their seats, strange music

filled the hall. At first, it sounded like a mixture of discorded instruments, but soon the melody started pulsing in her veins.

"What's happening?" she asked Zavir.

"Now," he said, kissing her shoulder, "we dance. But first, I have an announcement to make."

"That you're claiming me as charl?"

"No." His dark eyes filled with warmth. "That you accepted me as your cheren."

"Isn't it the same?"

"There was a time I believed so, but I was wrong." Getting to his feet, he pulled her with him. "Will you dance with me?"

"Always, but it's nice of you to ask."

"From now on," he whispered in her ear, "I'll keep on asking."

She looked up at his handsome face, seeing everything she could've ever wanted and hoped for in the depths of his eyes. "Then the answer will always be yes."

His reply was to lift her off her feet, inviting a squeal. When he carried her to the dance floor, she wrapped her arms around his neck and pressed her lips to his, forgetting for a moment they had an audience.

"Tell me something beautiful, kitten," he said, his gaze drinking in her face.

"I love you, Zavir."

His lips tilted in a sexy way. "I was hoping you'd say that."

~ THE END ~

Acknowledgments

All credit for the technology and physical attributes of the Krinar World used in this story goes to Anna Zaires and Dima Zales, with special reference to advanced nanotechnology, transport pods, Krinar dwellings and their unique characteristics, as well as Lenkarda, the Krinar Center in Costa Rica.

Thank you once again, Anna, for letting fans like me write in your Krinar World!

Also by Charmaine Pauls

Standalone Novels

(Enemies-to-Lovers Dark Romance)

Darker Than Love

(Second Chance Romance)

Catch Me Twice

———

Diamond Magnate Novels

(Dark Romance)

Standalone Novel

Beauty in the Broken

Diamonds are Forever Trilogy

Diamonds in the Dust (19 May 2020)

Diamonds in the Rough (14 July 2020)

Diamonds are Forever (15 September 2020)

———

The Loan Shark Duet

(Dark Mafia Romance)

Dubious

Consent

Box Set

———

The Age Between Us Duet

(Older Woman Younger Man Romance)

Old Enough

Young Enough

Box Set

———

Krinar World Novels

(Futuristic Romance)

The Krinar Experiment

The Krinar's Informant

———

About the Author

Charmaine Pauls was born in Bloemfontein, South Africa. She obtained a degree in Communication at the University of Potchefstroom and followed a diverse career path in journalism, public relations, advertising, communications, photography, graphic design, and brand marketing. Her writing has always been an integral part of her professions.

After relocating to Chile with her French husband, she fulfilled her passion to write creatively full-time. Charmaine has published novels as well as short stories and articles since 2011. Two of her short stories were selected for publication in an African anthology from across the continent by the International Society of Literary Fellows in conjunction with the International Research Council on African Literature and Culture.

When she is not writing, she likes to travel, read, and rescue cats. Charmaine currently lives in Montpellier with her husband and children. Their household is a linguistic mélange of Afrikaans, English, French and Spanish.

Join Charmaine's mailing list
https://charmainepauls.com/subscribe/

Join Charmaine's readers' group on Facebook
http://bit.ly/CPaulsFBGroup

Read more about Charmaine's novels and short stories on

https://charmainepauls.com

Connect with Charmaine

Facebook
http://bit.ly/Charmaine-Pauls-Facebook

Amazon
http://bit.ly/Charmaine-Pauls-Amazon

Goodreads
http://bit.ly/Charmaine-Pauls-Goodreads

Twitter
https://twitter.com/CharmainePauls

Instagram
https://instagram.com/charmainepaulsbooks

BookBub
http://bit.ly/CPaulsBB

Made in the USA
Middletown, DE
11 October 2020